P9-ECN-143

250

KATERI TEKAKWITHA, MOHAWK MAID

KATERI TEKAKWITHA

MOHAWK MAID

by

EVELYN M. BROWN

illustrated by

LEONARD EVERETT FISHER

VISION BOOKS

FARRAR, STRAUS AND CUDAHY, NEW YORK

BURNS AND OATES, LONDON

COPYRIGHT © 1958 BY EVELYN M. BROWN
LIBRARY OF CONGRESS CATALOG CARD
NUMBER 58–6840

Fourth Printing , October 1961

VISION BOOKS
IS A DIVISION OF
FARRAR, STRAUS & CUDAHY, INC.
PUBLISHED SIMULTANEOUSLY IN CANADA BY
AMBASSADOR BOOKS, LTD., TORONTO.
MANUFACTURED IN THE U.S.A.

To my dear Mother

Nihil Obstat:
Rt. Rev. Msgr. Peter B. O'Connor
Censor Librorum

Imprimatur:
✠ Most Reverend Thomas A. Boland, S.T.D.
Archbishop of Newark

The nihil obstat and imprimatur are official declarations that a book or pamphlet is free of doctrinal or moral error. No implication is contained therein that those who have granted the nihil obstat and imprimatur agree with the contents, opinions or statements expressed.

Contents

Author's Note

The first five chapters of this book are a careful weaving. The warp threads are the recorded facts, the main events in the life of Kateri and her mother. The weft threads are the minor incidents and characters of my own creation, based upon my discoveries of the customs, mentality, and folklore of the Iroquois people.

My sources for this work are too numerous to mention here. Outstanding among them is Father Lafitau's *Moeurs des Sauvages Amériquains*, written in old French.

As no one knows by what name Kateri was called in her early childhood, I invented the one Beautiful Day. All of the characters connected with the French campaign are real, including the old man under the canoe, whom I anticipated in the character of Grandfather, Agariata, and the Bâtard Flammand, though the name of Bright Feather is my own invention. Historians are not agreed on the order in which the Mohawk castles were taken; I have based my own account on that of Thomas Chapais.

The second half of the book keeps very close to the written records of Kateri. Here and there, in order to paint her against her own crude and colorful background, I have synchronized actual events in her life with tribal customs and superstitions.

I should perhaps explain that the name Kanawaki is Mohawk for Gandawagué, the simplified spelling of the French name Gandaouagué. In order to avoid confusion, I used two names for the two successive village sites.

Foreword

On Fifth Avenue, amid the hum of the great city of New York, is one of the most touching testimonies to the abiding power of love and joy in the world today. It is the bronze statuette of Kateri Tekakwitha, a young Iroquois girl born 300 years ago in an obscure longhouse. Featured in leather tunic and beads, she stands in a niche on one of the doors of St. Patrick's Cathedral in the glorious company of St. Patrick, St. Joseph, St. Isaac Jogues, Mother Cabrini, and Mother Seton.

To her title of Lily of the Mohawks, given to her by loving hearts, the Pope has added the one of Venerable. For great minds at the Vatican are studying the life of this little Mohawk maid who could neither read nor write, not only because of the records of her holiness, but because of the many miracles of healing attributed to her prayers.

The story of Kateri Tekakwitha is a love story in the true sense of the word. But its first chapters begin before her birth in the thrilling story of another little girl who became her mother. My book, therefore, opens with the story of Kahenta, captive and wife in an alien country, whose faithfulness to God and life of constant prayer won for her the reward of a daughter who may soon be proclaimed to all the world as a canonized saint.

1. The Captive

IT WAS THE MONTH WHEN THE HAIR OF
the deer turns to a burnished red. The early morning sun was scattering gold sequins over the
mighty St. Lawrence River. Blue smoke curled
lazily from cone-shaped wigwams that pointed up-
ward among the tall trees.

Kahenta thought there had never been a love-
lier day for a fishing trip. She was going up the
river with a party of Algonquin Indians to make

a bush net. There was a glow in her face as she tripped joyously along in her deerskin moccasins, a little behind the four men and a little ahead of the only other woman in the party, an old squaw.

Like the other girls of her tribe, she carried her slim young body with a nymphlike grace. She wore a plain white cotton blouse that she had learned to sew for herself at the French mission, and a skirt of dressed deerskin. Her long straight black hair, glossy with bear grease, was caught about the head with a narrow band of brightly colored wampum beads and hung down her back in tied bunches.

Suddenly the old squaw stood dead in her tracks and spat on the ground. "Iroquois dogs!" she exclaimed. There were bad things in her stomach today and she needed words to give vent to them.

A mangy dog looked up at her and barked in sympathy.

Kahenta laid down the poles she had been carrying and ran back to the old woman.

"You are tired, Grandmother!" she said kindly. "May I carry your basket for you?" She reached up for the burden strap. "I can sling the *happis* round my neck and carry yours in front as well as mine behind."

But the old woman waved her aside. "There's nothing but twine and a cold leg of goose in it, girl," she said. She pointed a rheumatic brown

finger at the high log stockade that made a pro-
tecting belt around the French fort of Trois-
Rivières. "It was that sight which tired me!" she
said. "How long ago was it, girl—three summers?
—when we lay all night long on our bellies inside
the fort listening to the thundersticks belching
fire and the screams of the wounded and the
dying."

Kahenta remembered. The French had let the
Indian Christian women and children take shelter
inside the fort during an Iroquois raid. This pagan
woman had long been a loyal friend of Kahenta's
family and had chosen to remain with them in the
Christian settlement even though she did not hold
by their faith.

The old woman chuckled. The frost of many
winters was on her head, and when she laughed
there were gaps in her mouth where teeth had
once been. "They got it that time, those Iroquois,
for all the guns they got from the paleface broadbreeches! Traded with the furs they'd stolen
from us Algonquins, too!"

The girl was silent. Talk about the Iroquois
always reminded her of a scene back in her
childhood. Suddenly she looked up and asked,
"Where is Ossernenon, Grandmother?"

"Ossernenon." The old squaw raised a work-
worn hand and passed it over her wrinkled forehead. "Ossernenon . . ." She pointed vaguely
over the tops of some wigwams. "It's way off

down yonder in Iroquois country," she said, "many nights' journey from here. What made you think of Ossernenon?"

Kahenta made no reply. In her mind she was remembering a pair of hands cruelly bitten and cut and burned by the Iroquois at Ossernenon. They were the hands of the blackrobe, Father Jogues, whom the Indians called Ondessonk. She had seen him only once—at the mission when he passed through Trois-Rivières four years after his torture. Never would she forget the sight of that holy man, nor how the Indians had wept and knelt and kissed his pitiful hands.

The old woman went on grumbling to herself. "It's the village of the Mohawks, the fiercest of the lot. *Makwa*, we Algonquins call them, because they get fat like the bear eating up all the other tribes around them. There are hundreds of those Iroquois down there at Ossernenon, and they say they have more than 300 guns."

Those poor hands, Kahenta was still thinking. But what had touched her most of all was that Ondessonk had returned to the same place to tell his tormentors about the Great Brave Jezos Who came to earth to die for love of them. That must be what the blackrobe meant when he talked of loving one's enemies. But could she, Kahenta, ever love the Iroquois?

The old squaw ceased muttering and glanced at her young companion. How silent the girl was!

Most Indian girls of her age were as full of conversation as a fall sunflower is full of seeds, but this one seemed to live in a world of her own. She was a good girl, and clever with her fingers, but sometimes as empty of words as a shell flute.

"Kahenta," she said at last, "if my old eyes didn't deceive me, wasn't that a fine young brave with a deer on his back who went into your wigwam last evening?"

The girl flushed. She hoped the men in front hadn't heard.

"Yes, Grandmother," she said softly, smiling from pleasure and shyness.

"Where are your bracelets and earrings, girl?" asked the old woman sharply. There was an echo of a scold in her voice, for she had not yet digested the Iroquois. But there was tenderness in her face as she looked at the girl beside her.

Kahenta glanced down at her bare arms and reached with her free hand for the lobe of one ear.

"I forgot to put them on, Grandmother," she said.

"Forgot them! A girl of your age has no business to forget to make herself pretty for a young man. You spend too much time in church praying on those beads of yours. Beads were meant to decorate a girl's body, not to pray on. And why do you think your mother pierced your ears when you were in the cradle, if it wasn't for earrings?"

She jerked the basket from her back and laid it

on the ground, fumbling in it for a small object tied up in a piece of clean birch bark. Carefully she undid the packet and drew out a pair of beautiful scarlet shell earrings.

"Oh, Grandmother!" cried the girl. "How kind of you!"

"I've been saving them for you," said the old woman, "till you were of an age to marry. They'll bring you luck in love."

She's as much of a matchmaker as my mother, thought Kahenta, when the old woman fastened first one, and then the other, ornament in the girl's ears.

There were no old maids among the Indians. An Indian girl married or starved. While her mother and this old friend were plotting for a fine hunter to bring in meat, she, Kahenta, was dreaming of papooses. What a beautiful day that would be, she thought, when she had a little bright-eyed papoose of her very own to fasten onto her back when she went out to the fields or down the river! Her heart grew warm and soft at the mere thought.

The fire of many summers, and the wisdom of generations of Indian women, were in Grandmother's eyes as she looked into Kahenta's young face. "Remember this, girl," she said. "A man wants more than a hard worker in a squaw. He likes to see his woman well dressed. And not with French baubles like this!" She tugged at a chain the girl was wearing around her neck under her blouse.

"That's not a French bauble, Grandmother," said the girl. "It's a crucifix. The blackrobe gave it to me. He said, 'Wear this, Kahenta, to remind you . . .'"

"Hurry, girl!" cried the old woman. "See, the men are already down at the canoes."

They quickened their pace and arrived just as the canoes were launched. The men went back to pick up the bows and arrows and clubs that they had left on the bank. As it was high summer, their coppery bodies were bare to the waist. From beaded belts bulged tomahawk and knife, and a tobacco pouch or fire bag swung at the hips. They were proud, erect and courteous like the other men of the Algonquin tribe. Because they were praying Indians, there was no conceit or haughtiness in their bearing.

Pingwi reached out a hand to help the old squaw into the large canoe.

"Dreaming of Iroquois, Grandmother?" he asked teasingly.

The old woman grunted. "If I'd dreamt of an Iroquois, I wouldn't have put my old nose outside of my wigwam," she retorted. "And what else are you dreaming of, going out to fish, armed to the teeth? All you want is a little war paint!"

Pingwi laughed. "Oh, those weapons are only in case a fat bear or a deer comes down to the river for a drink." It would spoil Grandmother's fishing trip to let her know what they had heard last night. A passing Huron had told them that down near Quebec a woman and her niece had been scalped in plain daylight while they were working in their garden. The Iroquois had slipped away into the forest before anyone realized what had happened.

"What's that?" cried Kahenta suddenly, pointing to three black dots on the horizon.

"Hurons," said one of the men quickly, but his tone was uneasy.

All eyes scanned the great shining highway of water as three canoes came rapidly toward them.

Grandmother said nothing and saw nothing, so tightly were her eyes screwed up in an effort to see. Beads of sweat pearled on her forehead and trickled down her furrowed cheeks. Her heart flumped inside her like a fish caught in a net.

Kahenta reached inside a little pocket of her skirt and fingered her rosary beads.

The three canoes came closer and closer. Men could be seen in them now.

"*Ouae! Ouae!*" came cries from the nearest one. They were the voices of their allies, friendly Huron voices raised in a salute. They drew nearer, heading for the French fort. In the midst of the Indians, and among bales of furs, was a tall, gaunt figure in black, a Jesuit missionary returning to his flock.

Pingwi, who understood the Huron language, exchanged a word with them as they went past. They had been paddling all night long, he said, in order to get their furs down the river under cover of darkness.

The old woman's body, which had been tense as a taut string, sank back into its customary curves.

"Safe enough we are in the day," she observed, as she settled herself in the canoe with a sigh of relief. "Those Iroquois are like frogs in a pond. They do all their croaking at night when it's quiet and dark. Let a leaf rustle, or a twig crack, and—flop! Down they all go under water!"

Everyone laughed. There was a special flavor to Grandmother's speeches.

The large, birch-bark canoe, containing three men and the old woman, arrowed out from the shore. Kahenta and Pingwi came after in a small one.

They crossed the St. Lawrence River and then turned off into one of the small tributaries. From here they could see no wigwams nor any other sign of human beings.

A pleasant dreaminess came over Kahenta as she paddled down between living walls of forest. Water had always enchanted her. She loved to look down into the river and see the broken reflections of clouds and trees slide past her as she skimmed along. There were the somber ranks of cedar and pine, the gayer green of elm, birch, and maple, and, here and there, trembling in the troubled surface of the water, a wild cherry with its swarms of snow-white blossoms.

They had been paddling for some time when suddenly the cry of a wild duck, sweet and savage and full of water loneliness, came from a reedy marsh.

Seeing the large canoe stop, Kahenta and Pingwi also back-paddled to a standstill. A wild duck was tasty meat for empty stomachs, and some of the party had not yet eaten that day.

All eyes were searching the rushes along the shore, but no bird could be seen.

The call came again. It was the cry of a bird for her mate.

Slowly the big canoe began to advance nearer to the place from which the sound had come. When the craft was within twenty feet of the shore, the cry came again. One of the men drew his bow, ready for the instant the bird would make its appearance.

Very cautiously the canoe inched nearer and nearer.

Suddenly from a distant point of land a wild duck came winging toward them. Then, catching sight of the Indians, it veered off. They could see by the green head with the white collar that it was the male bird.

Still no female bird appeared. The breeze had

died down. Perfect stillness hung over wood and water. Then a wild quacking and squawking came from the marsh—the panicky sound of a bird caught in the underbrush.

The canoe shot ashore into the middle of the reeds.

At the same instant a wild, bloodcurdling cry shattered the stillness as three Iroquois, hideous with war paint, sprang into view. One seized the canoe and held it. With the speed of an eagle pouncing on its prey, and before anyone could take a paddle stroke or draw a bow, two of the warriors seized the hair of two Algonquin men. With a single deft stroke of the tomahawk, they sliced off their scalps. There followed the dull shock of metal on scalp bone.

Throwing aside his bow, the third Algonquin warrior leaped on the back of the Iroquois holding the canoe. He fell back and the two rolled together among the reeds. The canoe shot away from the shore, jolting the old squaw onto her face. She lay there on the bottom of the canoe, whimpering with terror.

Nothing could be seen now but a violent thrashing of reeds where the Algonquin and the Iroquois were locked in fight.

Pingwi plunged his paddle into the water to go to the rescue of the others. The canoe spun around and was just about to head for the shore when there was a loud report from a gun. A

bullet passed so close to Kahenta's ear that she
could hear it hum as it flew beyond her. A second
bullet tore a hole in the upper part of the frail
canoe.

The Iroquois with the gun dashed out of the
forest to get a closer shot. Two other warriors
followed him.

Pingwi dropped his paddle and seized his bow.
But before he could draw back the arrow, a third
bullet hit him in the temple. Without a moan he
slumped forward.

The firing ceased.

Kahenta was now alone in the canoe and might
have tried to get to safety. But the girl had only
one thought. She must go to the help of the old
woman whose canoe had drifted dangerously near
the shore. From where she was, she could not
see whether Grandmother was alive or dead.

She paddled desperately in the direction of the
large canoe. A dozen strokes of the paddle and
she had reached it. As she leaned over to touch
the old squaw, she saw at a glance that Grandmother was dead. She felt a sob rise in her breast
and, at the same moment, a rough hand seized
her long hair and lifted it above her head.

"Jezos!" It was a silent cry for help from the
depths of her heart. No sound escaped her lips.

But the blow of the tomahawk did not come.
Instead, she heard a loud command in a strange,
harsh tongue and looked up to see a plumed war-

rior thrust back an Iroquois into the water and toss his tomahawk after him.

Then he turned and looked down at her.

Kneeling on the floor of her canoe, her hands now clasped in front of her, at first she did not see the face bent over her, nor the eyes full of curiosity and amazement. Her gaze was inward, fixed on the Great Spirit Who was her refuge.

His voice called her to attention. He was speaking to her in that rough, sharp tongue so different from the soft Algonquin speech. At once he saw that she could not understand.

Like the eyes of a deer caught in a thicket, her black eyes, calm but questioning, met his now with level gaze. Meekness and shyness were in those eyes, and fear, and the courage to face it.

And we call men women when they are cowards, he was thinking. If all women were like this one, the braves would have little to boast of!

For a full minute the Tortoise Chief studied the face of his captive. What was there in this Indian girl that he had never before met in any other woman of his, or another, tribe?

She dropped her eyes before his inquisitive stare. But the image of her captor was stamped upon her mind in every detail. She could see the little cap with the three eagle's feathers caught in a silver tube, the piercing eyes, the daubs of scarlet, black, and green paint on forehead, cheeks, chin, and nose. Was there hate or pity, scorn or

revenge, in that masklike face? It was impossible
to tell.

For an instant she glanced up again. She saw
the eagle feathers waving back and forth, back and
forth in the breeze.

2. Little White Deer

IT SEEMED TO KAHENTA THAT SHE HAD BEEN
traveling for many, many moons. As she got
farther and farther away from her home and
family, there were often tears in her heart. But
she walked with head high, eyes brave and resolute, a young girl all alone in the midst of the
Iroquois army. Instead of just a handful of men,
there were now nearly a hundred. They seemed to
come together by magic. By signs on trees, by

footprints that no paleface could ever see, or by imitating the song of a bird—a quail or rook by day, an owl by night—the scattered bands of warriors could find each other even in the thickest forest.

Twelve more prisoners had been brought in. All were Hurons and all men. What had become of Pingwi, Kahenta wondered. Had he been killed in the fight with the Iroquois? She thought of Grandmother as she had seen her lying dead in the bottom of the canoe. How she hoped that the old woman had had a moment of consciousness in which to wish for Christian baptism. The blackrobe had said that even a great desire for it was enough.

All day long they tramped through the forest, or traveled in elm-bark Iroquois canoes up rivers, past endless islands crowned with nut and oak. When they trekked along woodland paths, they went in single Indian file. Kahenta's place was just behind the last Huron prisoner. The first day she had been bound with willow withes as had the rest. After that, by order of the Tortoise Chief, she had been untied and allowed to walk free.

Every evening before sunset the Iroquois chose a place to encamp, usually on the bank of a river or stream. The other prisoners were bound hand and foot to posts driven firmly into the ground. When Kahenta saw their extreme misery, their open wounds, their flesh devoured by mosquitos, she was glad that none of her companions had been taken prisoner with her. Her own bed was a mattress of spruce or hemlock boughs placed a stone's throw from the sleeping army.

As the language spoken by both the Iroquois and the Hurons was the same, and Kahenta knew no word of it, few paid any attention to her except the Tortoise Chief. Even he seldom noticed her directly. But often she felt his eyes watching her as she helped drag a canoe to the water, or gave a hand in skinning and preparing the game brought in by the younger men who went in search of food. She had been used to doing these things at home and had always found joy in work. Now, as a prisoner, she discovered that it helped drive away sorrow and care to keep her hands occupied. With nimble fingers she could prepare and roast several pieces of deer or raccoon in less time than it took any of the men to do one.

She had another reason for doing these things. She was hoping to get mercy for the Huron prisoners, some of whom she was sure were Christians. It showed in many small and big ways—the expressions on their faces, their gentle manners, and their quiet courage which was so different from the mocking bravado of the pagans. Now and then she had heard the notes of hymns that she knew in her own tongue. She thought that if she worked well and willingly, she might be able to save them from the terrible tortures that other

Huron and Algonquin prisoners had suffered for their faith.

The thought of torture for herself had seldom troubled her, for her own tribe and the Hurons never tortured their women prisoners. Once, however, it did enter her mind. They had stopped at the mouth of the great Richelieu River to record the army's victories in picture writing on a tree. On this same tree, from which a large section of bark had been cut away, the facts of the expedition had been painted on the army's way out.

A crude tortoise, drawn with a piece of charcoal, was at the top. Underneath that were signs to show the places to which they were going, the number of canoes and men, and the tribes and villages they were going to attack. Kahenta could not read these, though she had often heard about them. What she did know was that, on the return journey, the Iroquois showed, by a few strokes of charcoal and red paint, what they were going to do with prisoners. A red skull meant slow torture by fire. A little hook, like the willow withes used for binding prisoners, stood for ones who would be made slaves.

Her heart seemed to rise to her throat as she watched the Tortoise Chief take charcoal and red paint from a pouch to mark up the fate of the thirteen prisoners. First he drew two canoes homeward bound. There followed some rapid strokes with the red paint, and five fiery scalps stood in a line. Under these, with a piece of charcoal, he began sketching in the black hooks. Kahenta counted them on her fingers. There were seven in all. One prisoner had been left out.

Perhaps it is I, she thought, since I am the only one not bound. But what this might mean she did not know.

After that, they spent many more days in weary travel. She was grateful for the nights. Alone and unseen in God's great wigwam, she could say her prayers. Above her was the moon, like a radiant host around which stars blazed like candles on an unseen altar. For heaven to her was not a vast hunting ground filled with wild game, but a place where the Great Spirit lived with His Son Jezos and the Mother of His Son, the most pure Virgin. It comforted her in her loneliness to think that, though she could not see where she was going, the Creator of all things could see, and this alone was safety. The little rosary beads slipped one by one through her fingers and, when she came to the mystery of the crown of thorns, with all her heart she prayed for courage.

At last one day Kahenta felt that they were nearing the end of their long journey. In the scorching heat of the afternoon the army came to a halt for a rest on the banks of a broad river which she heard the soldiers call the Mohawk. No game had been brought in that day. This was a sign that they were nearing their village and expected a great feast.

Many of the warriors sat around now, rapidly plucking out the hair from their chins and fore-heads with mussel shells or wire tweezers which they carried in their fire bags. When the surface of the skin was smooth enough, they began to apply fresh paint. That's for the triumphal return, thought Kahenta, and to terrify their prisoners by hiding their feelings and thoughts from them. She had often seen the men of her own tribe do this.

She got up and strolled among the trees. A short distance away in a clearing she found a pool. Lonely and sick for home, she sat down beside it. Vivid blue dragonflies darted among the golden water lilies that lay on its quiet surface. Mingled with the wild chorus of birds' voices, she could hear the laughter and chatter of a little spring that flowed into the pool. How glad she had always been for the company and conversation of the wild things—for the birds and beasts, for the streams and rivers which, with their silver fingers, trace out a path for the Indians as sure as any map drawn on paper by a wise geographer.

As she sat looking into the pool, the reflection of a tall man wearing a cluster of eagle's feathers suddenly appeared beside her own. A voice said, "*Sago!*" It was the Iroquois greeting; the Tortoise Chief was standing over her. He opened a small sack of finely ground corn flour which all the warriors carried on their backs and, making a sign to her to open her palm, poured some into her hand. Indian fashion, she put it on her tongue. Cupping her hand in the water, she brought it to her mouth and swallowed the mixture. It was sweet and satisfying, and one could go for many hours without other food.

The girl made a gesture of thanks, but she knew that this might not be kindness on his part. The Huron pagans feasted the prisoners they meant to torture the most cruelly.

Suddenly the chief squatted on the grass beside her and took out a piece of freshly peeled bark and a stick of charcoal. He signaled to her to watch him. With a few bold strokes of the charcoal he drew a tortoise, held it up before her, and pointed to himself. Then he pointed to her, turned the bark over to the blank side, and passed it to her with the charcoal.

She felt the blood rise to her cheeks and flush over her neck. He was asking her to tell him what her family crest, or totem, was. Could it mean that he thought of marrying her? If an Indian girl's totem was the same as the man's, marriage between them was forbidden. Would it be the same for a captive?

How could she, an Algonquin girl and a Christian, ever bring herself to marry an enemy and a pagan?

An acute temptation came to her. She would hide the truth from him. She would draw a tortoise.

She lifted the charcoal. Her fingers hovered over the bark. A tiny head, a big top-heavy body, and four silly little legs. It would be so simply and quickly done, and the question would be settled forever.

But the voice of conscience spoke to her. A Christian would gain nothing by telling a lie. She had prayed for protection and now she must act truthfully, no matter what happened.

Slowly she drew a deer with large wistful eyes and leaf-shaped ears.

He took the bark from her. A light flashed in his dark brown eyes and all his teeth showed in a broad smile.

Full of shyness and confusion, she bent over the pool to pluck a lily. The reflection of the man beside her disappeared. In the clear, limpid water she saw only her own image—her hair no longer shining with bear grease, her blouse rumpled and torn—and, remembering Grandmother's words, she felt glad that she was so poorly dressed. At that moment she caught sight of the scarlet earrings. Reaching up, she tugged at first one and then the other till they came out. But she could not bring herself to throw them away. They were a souvenir of an old and loyal friend. As she slipped them into her pocket, she glanced up to see the army moving down to the river.

Iroquois and prisoners took their places in the canoes. Was it by accident or by order that her own was in the same canoe as that of the Tortoise Chief?

During the journey down the Mohawk River, the future seemed quite unreal to Kahenta. To be moving along on a swift dancing current scattered her thoughts as water divides sunlight into a million sparkling diamonds.

From time to time the Indians broke into song. The pagan prisoners stood in the canoes and sang and danced as was expected of them. In the brief silences the Christians sang their hymns.

At last Kahenta caught the first glimpse of the great twenty-foot triple stockade that circled the Iroquois village. The sun was setting behind it. In its crimson light she could see a swarm of canoes coming out to meet the army.

It was the moment of great triumph. Scalps were held aloft. The hair streamed out on the wind like gruesome banners of victory. Paddles struck the water, beating a rhythmic pattern for the stamping of feet and the slapping of thighs.

As they drew nearer to the village, the victors took up the song. Every verse ended with their wild war whoop, "Aw! . . . Oh!" from a low note to a high one, the last being held as long as there was breath in their bodies. There was one cry for each scalp taken.

Crowds of people thronged the shore to welcome the returning army. Dogs barked with excitement. Some of the women threw off their clothes, plunged into the water, and swam to the canoes. Seizing the scalps, they swam back with them, waving them above their heads and shouting with glee. The scalps would be dried and painted and kept as trophies.

Kahenta, who had been brought up among Christian Indians and had never come close to such sights, was filled with disgust and pity.

Under the staring eyes of men, women, and children who pressed close to get a better view of the prisoners, she climbed the steep hill to the village and passed through the door of the huge wooden stockade.

Never had she seen so many houses in all her life, nor such big ones. She had heard the Iroquois called the people of the longhouse. Now she saw for herself the great wood-framed lodges walled and covered with bark, with their arched roofs.

As she was looking around her, bewildered, a young woman came from the crowd and made a sign to Kahenta to follow. She eyed the Algonquin girl curiously from time to time as she led her through the village and up to one of the big lodges.

They entered by way of a shedlike room filled

with firewood, jugs for carrying water, food in bark barrels, and baskets of corn husks.

Beyond that, all Kahenta could see at first in the dim light was a long corridor reaching from end to end of the building and spotted at intervals with fires that glowed in shallow, bowl-shaped hearths.

As her eyes got used to the half-dark, she could see dried pumpkins and bunches of corn braided by the husks hanging from the rafters. On either side of the corridor, and a foot or two above the floor, was a low platform covered with mats and furs. The girl Anastasia motioned to her to squat on one of these.

Since Indian hospitality, even for a helpless enemy, meant food, the Iroquois girl brought Kahenta a wooden bowl filled with *sagamite*, and a wooden spoon. Making a sign for Kahenta to help herself to more food left on the fire, she placed a dish of corn bread and fruit beside the Algonquin girl and slipped out of the longhouse to join the crowd.

Two sleepy hounds jumped off one of the platforms and came over to her as she ate. After a few mouthfuls of food, she could take no more and set the dish down before them.

Now, more than ever, loneliness crept into her heart.

Away in the distance the war kettles, or drums,

throbbed like a great heartbeat in the night, keeping time for the choruses and dances. She could hear men's voices rise in a song of triumph and terror. When they ceased, the women took up the strain in full, clear notes. At the end of each song came a yell like a far-off clap of thunder.

Kahenta got up and went to the door.

Away at one end of the village she could see fiery points of light and columns of flame. Were they torturing the Christians?

She tried to remember the eyes of the chief. What were they saying to her? What should she do if he asked her to become his wife? If only she were a man and could die in the flames and go to paradise praying to the Great Spirit! If only the blackrobe were here to tell her what she should do!

She sat down again and took out her rosary beads. The Mother of Jezos was a girl like herself. She would understand and show her what to do. As the beads slipped beneath her fingers, she remembered a picture she had once seen of the Virgin holding her Child in her arms. And she looked just my age, Kahenta thought. Then the picture changed and she saw a young man with a deer on his back, the Christian that her mother had chosen for her.

She felt the crucifix under her blouse. What had the blackrobe said? "This is to remind you,

Kahenta, that all your work, your joys, your sorrows and sacrifices can be a present for the Great Spirit of Love."

This, too? she wondered. Was this, then, the sacrifice that the Great Spirit asked of her? She tried to bring her mind back to her prayers, but again she saw only the Virgin Mother with her Child.

I shall have a child if I marry, she thought, and perhaps a blackrobe will come here one day and baptize my child and he will grow up to be a good Christian and change the people of this village. Her fingers were on the large bead. ". . . Thy will be done on earth as it is . . . Perhaps, if I live my religion well, my husband . . ." But she could not finish the thought. Worn out with the long journey, she lay down and fell fast asleep.

She was awakened by a hand shaking her arm. She sat up and rubbed her eyes, wondering where she was.

A woman with a basket and a bundle of clothes on her arm was bending over her. Eagerly she was fingering Kahenta's rosary. "Then you are a Christian?" she asked.

Kahenta felt her whole heart open with joy. For the first time in weeks a woman was speaking to her and in her own language.

"Yes," she said. "I am a captive."

"I, too, am a Christian Algonquin," said the woman. "I have not seen a rosary for a long, long time—not since Ondessonk was here."

"Ondessonk!" cried the girl. "Then I am at Ossernenon!"

"Yes," said the woman. "Ondessonk was killed here nine summers ago. There has never been a blackrobe here since then."

She laid her basket and the bundle of clothes on the mat. "You must put on these clothes now," she said, lifting up a magnificent white-tanned buffalo dress richly ornamented with colored beads and porcupine quills.

Kahenta obeyed, taking off her own shabby clothes and letting the woman help her into the dress.

"But this is for a princess," said the girl uneasily. White among the Indians was worn only for very important ceremonies. "Who sends these clothes to me?"

"They are the gift of the Tortoise Chief," said the woman. "He wishes to marry you. His wife died in the month of the running sap, and you are adopted to take her place."

So soon, thought Kahenta. She was silent as she tugged at the handsome beaded leggings and tied them above her knees.

"Don't be afraid," said the woman, slipping the embroidered beaded moccasins onto the girl's feet. "The Great Spirit has given you very special protection. Believe me, marriage is the best thing that can ever happen to a Christian girl captured by the Iroquois. I am married to a pagan myself."

She opened her basket, took out an antler comb and a small box of grease, and began to arrange the girl's hair. Beautiful bracelets, earrings, and a dab of rouge on Kahenta's cheeks put the finishing touches to her grooming.

"We can't talk longer now," said the woman. "Here, put your rosary into the top of your legging. I am to show you where to meet him."

Together they went out into the night. A full moon made milky pools and charcoal shadows among lodges and trees.

At the door of the stockade the woman stopped. "You see that great spreading oak tree down by the bend in the river?"

The girl nodded.

"It's a favorite meeting place for lovers." She pressed the girl's arm. "Have no fear, Little Sister," she said. "The Tortoise Chief is cruel in war but kind in love, and you will have happiness in your children. May the Great Spirit lighten your cross."

Kahenta's answer was a little squeeze of her hand.

The woman Koincha watched her as she went

down the hill, light-footed and graceful as a young deer, until she was just a little shadow against the moonlit river that hurried by, laced in strands of silver.

3. Beautiful Day

IT WAS THE YOUTH OF THE YEAR. ONCE AGAIN the maples lifted their jade, tufted branches to the sky and the leaf of the white oak was the size of a mouse's ear.

In the evening, at twilight, the whippoorwill called out her Indian name, "Wekolis! Wekolis!" The clear, round, rollicking notes rang through the woods like an invitation to joy. In their longhouses the Indians lifted their heads to listen. "It is time to plant the corn," they said.

The earth lay rich and brown, ready to receive the precious seed. Chattering like magpies, the young squaws trooped out of the stockade with their babies on their backs and their baskets of seed in their hands and took their places in the fields.

Anastasia was there, and Koincha, and other friends of Kahenta's, but Kahenta was not there.

She was at home today, her first baby lying beside her.

"She's all mine," Kahenta thought, as she looked down at the tiny round head with its sprinkling of damp, black hair. Even if her husband tired of her one day and sent her away, the child would be hers forever by right of Indian law.

The Tortoise Chief sat on the edge of the mat, touching the baby's crumpled fist with one finger and grinning from ear to ear.

"What shall we call her?" he asked.

Kahenta was silent for a moment. Even in the dim longhouse she could feel the rushing tide of spring. And because the sun shone golden as a dandelion in the open door, and because the birds were singing with all their hearts, and because she was happy as she had never before been happy in her captivity, she answered, "Waniseriio—Beautiful Day."

But no sooner had she given the name than her joy was mixed with sorrow.

"Blessed Mother of Jezos," her heart was crying, "please ask the Great Spirit to send a black-robe some day so that I may have my baby baptized. But if he never comes, may the tears in my heart count to make her truly a Christian."

Little did she dream that one day her child would bear the name of Tekakwitha and that centuries later, when the village of Ossernenon had disappeared and the footsteps of American children would be heard in the streets of Auriesville, New York, many many pilgrims would visit the place and would say, "This is where Tekakwitha was born."

As soon as Kahenta was strong enough to work with the other women and girls, she would wrap Beautiful Day in a woolen blanket, lace her to her cradle board, and carry the child on her back to the fields or out into the woods when she went to gather wild berries, roots, and nuts.

While she worked, Kahenta would hang the baby to the branch of a tree. Slung between earth and sky, Beautiful Day would sleep peacefully while the little birds perched beside her and the squirrels peeped at her with round-eyed wonder.

Now and then, when the laughter and talk of the women grew louder, the baby would waken and mingle her cries with the songs of the birds.

Then her mother would go to her, and feed her, and say soft words to her in the Algonquin tongue.

As time passed and Beautiful Day grew into a round-faced, chubby little girl with nut-brown eyes, she began to make discoveries. She found that there were two worlds for her, her father's world and her mother's world. Her father was tall and sturdy as a young pine. He would pick her up in his great brown arms and toss her in the air till she screamed with delight and terror and seized his scalp lock in her two little fists.

Then the Tortoise Chief would laugh. When he laughed, his laughter filled the whole world, partly because he was happy and partly because he believed mightily in himself. For did not the Iroquois think that the American continent was one big island held up on the back of a tortoise? No chiefs were so important as the Tortoise Chiefs, and none for Beautiful Day more important than her own father—not even her Uncle Onsengongo, who was bigger and much older than her father and who had a great, heavy face and fierce, sad eyes.

But while Father's world was full of power, Mother's world was full of peace. For Mother was all kindness and gentleness, and being with her was like being beside a still pool at twilight. Beautiful Day wanted to please her father and to get his approval. With her mother, she was content just to grow as a daisy of the field grows, or as the wild rose opens its petals.

There were wonderful things for the little Indian girl to explore in the big longhouse. It was a three-fire lodge. That meant there were five families besides her own, two families to each fire. There was also an old man whom they all called Grandfather and who could only hobble, so bad was his rheumatism.

Beautiful Day was always eager to do little services for others and, as she was a sweet and loving child, everyone took to her and she felt welcome wherever she went. Sometimes, when the Tortoise family and the other family who shared their fire were eating together, the chief would pick up a bowl of *sagamite* and say, "Is there a good child who will take this food to Grandfather?" Beautiful Day would be the first to jump to her feet. Carefully she would take the bowl in her two little hands and go off with it, so joyous and gay to be helping out that she would scarcely notice the comments of the older folk: "Ah! see what a good child the Tortoise Chief has! That little girl is thinking of the time when she, herself, will be old and in need of help."

There was no quarreling in the longhouse, not even among the children, and yet there were no walls to separate the families—only a big closet at each end and on either side of the corridor. The closet belonging to the Tortoise Chief's

family was a happy hunting ground for Beautiful
Day. In it she slept on one of the shelves put
there as bunks for small children. But down below all sorts of exciting things were stored. Best
of all she loved to drag out her father's tomahawk.
It was gaily painted and decorated with beadwork, feathers, and fur, and made a fine toy
even if it was a little heavy.

In this closet, but out of reach of small hands,
Father kept his fine clothes. Most of the time
he dressed shabbily, like the other chiefs who
wanted to give the impression that they thought
little of themselves and gave much to the poor.
But when he had to go to a big council fire he
would dress up in his handsome beaver robe, wear
his fancy necklace of bear's claws, and put a crown
of mother-of-pearl beads on his head. Looking
up at him, his small daughter thought there never
had been a more superb man in all the world.

One day the little girl found the most wonderful of all toys in the closet. Lying on the shelf
opposite to hers was a tiny baby brother. From
that time on, the tomahawk was taken out less
often. During the day, when Little Brother lay on
the mat down below, she would sit by the hour
playing with him while Mother went about the
work of the house.

Dearest of all times to Beautiful Day were
those spent camping in the forest with her family
and the other Indians. First there was the sugar-

ing month when the whole village took to the woods where the maple trees were thickest. Together the men and women would build rough lodges. Then, while the mothers caught the sap from the trees and put it into kettles to make into syrup and sugar, the fathers would go out hunting fat bears.

Later on in the year they would all leave Ossernenon again and go to the woods to gather eggs and grown-up birds when the passenger pigeons were nesting. It delighted Beautiful Day to see the smooth, round eggs and feel them still warm beneath her fingers, but she never liked to see the dead birds brought in. Even as a child she couldn't bear to see anything hurt.

Again, between the time of the gathering of the golden corn and the month when the squirrels come out of their holes, the village would be nearly empty while family groups went off to their hunting camps in the woods. Then all the world would be hushed and white with snow and the stags would have dropped their horns. Father would be out all day long, and Beautiful Day would remain in the cabin with Baby Brother, snug in her dress of deerskin with the fur on the inside for warmth.

It was not until she was five years old that she began to feel how great the distance was between her father's world and her mother's.

Now there were times when she was afraid

of her father, for sometimes the power in him
would become all wild and reckless. She noticed
this most when he came home from trading with
the broadbreeches and had drunk the firewater
that they gave the Indians to make them foolish
so that they would sell their furs cheaper. Then
the light would die in her mother's face and it
would become still like a frozen pool. Although
Beautiful Day was still a very little girl, she knew
that her mother felt far away from her father's
world and, while she neglected nothing for his
comfort or pleasure, deep down in her heart she
pitied him.

There were so many differences between Father's world and Mother's world! When Father
was happy, he held his head high and put offer-
ings on the roof to the Sun God—corncobs, or a
string of wampum beads, or some tobacco. When
Mother was happy, she bowed her head and
seemed to shut a door between herself and all
the world. Then she would look more beautiful
and peaceful than ever.

Father went out to dances and would sometimes spend the whole day painting his face, but
Mother never went with him—not even when
the other women went out. Always she found
some good excuse for staying at home. "I must
bake extra bread in case the ambassadors come
this week," she would say, or, "I must finish the
moccasins I have been making for you." Then

her husband would be so pleased to have such a dutiful and loving wife that he would leave her without a word.

The brave and the proud came to see Father, but often Mother's visitors were the sick and the sad. And sometimes, when she went to see some sick woman who could not move from her mat, she would take Beautiful Day with her and give her some present to carry. The little girl noticed that faces always brightened at the sight of her gentle mother.

When her father came home from the wars, Beautiful Day was always eager to hear if he had been victorious. If so, she was full of gladness—not really, as he thought, because he had won glory. She was glad because she would have her mother all to herself, for Mother never went to join in the feasting nor to watch the torturing of prisoners. Early in the evening all the men, women and children, and even Grandfather, went out. The big longhouse was almost empty.

When Little Brother had been put to bed, Mother would often take her small daughter on her lap and sing her songs in a language that Father never spoke. And she would tell her in the Iroquois tongue about the Great Spirit who made all the lovely things around them—the birds, and flowers, and the little live squirrels that Beautiful Day wanted so much to catch for playthings.

She would tell her, too, about His Son, the Great Brave, who was tortured far worse than the prisoners Father brought home from the war, and how He bore it all for love.

Listening to her mother, the child would understand not with her head but with her heart, because to be folded in Mother's arms made love the nearest thing in all the world and the whole universe a safe place to live in.

Then her mother would take out her rosary beads and tell her about the Mother of the Great Brave. "A maid in blue," she would say, pointing to the blue beads in the little girl's moccasins, "and the most loving mother in all the world."

After that she would put the child to bed on her shelf opposite to Little Brother where she would fall asleep to dream of a maid in blue with a brown face just like her own mother's and smooth black hair with an eagle's feather in it.

Always and always Beautiful Day would belong to her Mother's world! But a sad day came when death visited both of her worlds.

It was in the month of the roasting ears of corn that all the sorrow came. One day her father lay on the mat tossing and turning and flushed with fever. Mother did not go to the fields that day. She came and went with bowls of steaming hot herbs and took notice of her children only to feed them and put them to bed.

In the middle of the night Beautiful Day woke up to hear a fearful noise. The longhouse was full of people. Women were shrieking and wailing at the tops of their voices. From her bunk she could see great shadows cast by the firelight on walls and ceiling and, among them, one more terrible than them all. It looked like a huge monster with horns and a long tail that swung back and forth. As it moved, it made a strange, rattling sound.

Terrified but curious, the child worked her way to the end of her bunk where she could look down on her father's and mother's mat. The great creature whose shadow she had seen was bending over her sick father. It was jet black and hairy like a bear and had long claws at the end of its feet. It breathed in her father's face, blew on his feet, and squirted medicines in his mouth and nose. All the time it did this, it shook a gourd filled with pebbles and dried beans to frighten away the evil spirit that was supposed to be the cause of the illness.

In the morning strange women were still wailing and shrieking, but now they were not crying for a living chief but for a dead one.

Even after the body was taken from the house, Beautiful Day could hear loud sounds of weeping outside in the village.

All day and all night the crying continued. Then people came into the house and took away all that her father had owned—his fine clothes from the closet, the tomahawk, and even the bowl from which he ate.

The chiefs of the village came, too, bringing a wampum belt of black and white beads to her mother. "This is to dry your tears," they said, but that very day Mother and Little Brother were both flushed with fever and lying on the mat together where Father had lain.

After that, Beautiful Day never saw her mother again, for she, herself, was sick with the smallpox.

No juggler was called in when her mother was ill, and there was no loud wailing in the house, not even when she died. Death that had pounced like an eagle on her pagan father laid a quiet and sheltering wing on her Christian mother.

Little Brother went, too, and that left only Beautiful Day of all the Tortoise Chief's family.

How long those days of illness seemed to the little girl as she lay burning with fever! Where was Mother? Where was Little Brother? Other hands came to bring her food or medicines. They were the hands of Koincha, or of Anastasia, never the hands she loved the most.

Sometimes she would cry for her mother, but her eyes were sick and the pain in them became worse when the tears gathered.

At last the day came when she could get up. How lonely the big longhouse was then! Even the people who had seemed so near to her now seemed far away, almost as though they belonged to another world altogether, as far away from hers as the farthest star in the sky.

Whom should she ask the question that lay in her heart? Grandfather was old and very wise. He would tell her what she wanted to know.

"Grandfather," she said one day after giving him a bowl of *sagamite*, "where is my mother? Where is Little Brother?"

Grandfather coughed, rubbed the sorer of his legs, and said, "They went off on a long journey, way down beyond the big pine forest."

Beautiful Day didn't ask again, partly because she was a good and patient child and partly because Grandfather's eyes had told her everything he didn't want to put into words.

After that there was a great stillness in her. She was as obedient as ever, and quick to help out whenever she could, only now there was a new shyness in her, for she was all alone and seemed no longer to belong to anyone.

Then one day Uncle Onsengongo stood towering over Beautiful Day. She stood still in the sunlight holding a small blanket across her eyes so that she did not see him clearly, but she felt his great bulk above her. She knew that the fierce, sad eyes were looking down on her.

"Is the daughter of the departed one then so timid?" he said, tugging at the corner of the blanket. It came away easily in his powerful hand.

"Look at me, child," he said. "A princess should wear her shawl like other girls—over her shoulders, not in front of her face."

She made a feeble attempt to smile and lifted her face toward him, but the instant she opened her eyes to look at him, they swam with tears and the lids dropped before them like frail curtains.

"They say that the illness has weakened her eyes," said her Aunt Teedah, who was standing beside him. She took the little girl by the hand and led her back into the longhouse.

"Look at me, child," said the uncle once again when they were inside.

He had taken the black and white wampum belt down from the rafter where it hung and was looking heavily from it to the child.

In the half-light of the lodge Beautiful Day lifted her face once again to his. The gentle, deep brown eyes, timid as a lost fawn's, opened to their full width and looked beseechingly into his own.

"What am I holding in my hand, Waniseriio?" he asked. He was standing a few feet from her.

She looked down in the direction of his hand, but made no answer. Then shyly she took two steps toward him. "The belt they brought my mother," she said quietly.

A long silence followed and then a satisfied

grunt came from somewhere very deep down inside Uncle Onsengongo.

"She will be like her mother," he said, "slim and graceful. The eyes are damaged but still beautiful."

Aunt Teedah put both her arms around the child. Her touch was kind, but greedy, for she had never had a child of her own. Beautiful Day felt farther away from her now than when she had been standing apart.

"You are to be our daughter now," her uncle was saying. "I am your father."

In the back of his great melancholy head he was picturing the husband he would get for her. The daughter of a chief would marry well, and this would mean plenty of food and care for his wife and himself in their old age.

"You will come with us?" he asked, not unkindly, laying his palm on her head.

"Yes . . . Father," she said, and, because he was very big and powerful, and because he was a Tortoise Chief like her father, she put a timid little hand into his big one.

4. Tekakwitha

"TEKAKWITHA! TEKAKWITHA!"

A little girl of ten, pounding corn under the shade of an oak tree, stood still and listened.

Had someone called her? Surely that mocking voice had come from behind one of the lodges. But, though she strained her ears, she could hear only the warbling of a hermit thrush and the excited chirping of little birds that flocked around her, eager for a tidbit.

She looked down lovingly at them. "Greedy children!" she cried, tossing them a handful of grain. "And now, little talebearers who fly so high and see so far, tell me, who called Tekakwitha?"

They fluttered all around her, almost brushing her with their tiny wings.

What a beautiful day it is! she thought. Then, suddenly, although the early morning sky was as clear as a glass bead and all the world was full of song, she felt as if a little cloud had gathered on the horizon.

No one ever calls me Beautiful Day any more, she thought wistfully, as she plunged her wooden pestle once more into the foamy grain. Someone very loving had called her that, but that was long, long ago. That was in another world.

Te-ka-kweeta. She repeated the name softly to herself. Never mind, she thought, and then, with a brave smile, she said aloud, "It's better than Bad Shoes!"

"What's better than Bad Shoes?" asked a teasing voice as a young Indian girl, a little older than Tekakwitha, jumped from behind the tree and caught her affectionately around the waist.

Tekakwitha started so violently that the pestle flew out of her upraised hands.

"What a scare you did give me, Anidas," she said, laughing. "How did you creep up without my hearing you?"

"That's easy enough with Tekakwitha!" teased the girl. "She is always so hard at work that she doesn't hear any farther than she sees. One would think you loved work! But tell me, now, what is better than Bad Shoes?"

"My name," said Tekakwitha, picking up her pestle and setting to work again. "It sounds like a busy woodpecker tapping on a tree!"

Both girls laughed merrily.

"Do you remember Bad Shoes, Anidas? The man whose corn-husk shoes were always coming apart?"

"I remember him," said Anidas. "He lived near our lodge when we were all down the river at Ossernenon before the plague drove us up here."

She squatted on the ground beside her companion. There was something about this frail, shy girl with the ready laughter that warmed Anidas' heart and made her want to be with her.

She sat still for a few minutes, lazily sucking a blade of grass and watching the spots of sunlight sift through the leaves and glint on her bracelets and rings.

"I wish they would start calling *me* another name," she said with a little pout of her painted lips. "Anidas, the skunk, is not my favorite animal!"

"When one likes the person, one likes the name," said Tekakwitha gently.

"I'd rather be called by the name they gave to
Occuna—Beloved Lover," said her companion,
"or, better still, Met by Love." Anidas looked up
dreamily into the branches of the great oak.
"Wouldn't you like to be called that, Tekakwitha?"

Tekakwitha's pestle paused in mid-air. She
brought it down thoughtfully under her chin.
"Met By Love," she said quietly, as a smile flick-
ered over her small face. For a moment she forgot that Anidas was there, for it seemed as though
something as fragile as a butterfly had opened
and closed its wings in her heart. Oh! how I
should like to be called that, she was thinking.
Her lips parted for a second as though to give
words to her thought but, suddenly catching sight
of Anidas, she closed them again and went on
pounding.

"It's true, Tekakwitha!" cried the girl, jump-
ing up and standing beside the low, hollowed-out
stump that her companion used for a mortar. "It
was a Seneca girl. One day she went to draw
water at a spring, and there she met the most
handsome brave in all the world. He fell in love
with her, and their life together was so happy
that ever after everyone called her Met By Love."

She patted her smooth hair coyly, for an Indian girl of eleven is nearly a woman.

Tekakwitha looked up at the sky. On clear
days like this her uncle came back early. It was

only on cloudy or rainy days that the wild game were abroad all day long.

"Do you see Great Pine up there on the hill, Anidas?" she asked. "When the sun stands over Great Pine my uncle will be back and as hungry as a hunter. I have all the bread to bake before he comes. Will you help me finish the pounding?"

"Of course I will, Favorite One," Anidas said. "That kind of work isn't meant for delicate arms like yours."

She picked up a pestle lying by the trunk of the tree and set up a wooden mortar next to Tekakwitha's. With a big ladle she scooped out half the corn mixture and put it into her mortar.

The two friends worked side by side. Up and down, up and down went the pestles as each girl pounded to the rhythm of her dreams.

Met By Love, Anidas was thinking. I like the son of Sganarady. I hope my mother picks him for me. But I'm afraid she favors that stupid son of the Bear Chief. He was eight years old before he could even catch a rabbit!

Met By Love, Tekakwitha was thinking. Some day . . . And then perhaps I'll have a new name. I shall no longer be Tekakwitha—the one blinded by light, the one who moves things before her. . . .

When the corn was ground fine enough to make into a dough, Tekakwitha ladled it from both mortars into a birch-bark container.

"I must go down to the gardens now," she said, picking up her basket.

As they left the shade of the tree and stepped out into the blazing August sunlight, she took her shawl from her shoulders and held it in front to shade her eyes.

By now the village was full of activity. Women were cooking meat or smoking hides out in the open.

A little group of girls was squatted on the ground playing a game. They had painted prune stones black on one side and were tossing them in the air from a plate of birch bark.

"Black side down!" cried one, holding the plate beneath it to catch it as it fell.

"It's brown side down!" shouted a chorus of voices.

Tekakwitha was glad when they passed through the door of the stockade. It always gave her a feeling of freedom to be out in the open fields with the Mohawk River running by and great stretches of wild country all around her. The sight of the rich and beautiful harvest—the crowded ranks of corn swelling to ripeness under the sun's rays, glossy pumpkins like harvest moons, juicy watermelons and squashes meekly squatting among their prickly vines—always filled her with joy. And the sunflowers! How she loved the tall glory of them!

"It will be Harvest Festival soon," said Anidas

eagerly, jigging about and waving her arms as though she were dancing. "What a pity your eyes are too poor to join in the dances, Tekakwitha!"

"But think how clumsy Tekakwitha would be!" laughed the other, picking up her skirt and pretending to tumble over a pumpkin. Both girls laughed gaily.

"You live like a little mole," said Anidas. "Couldn't you come to the tortures sometimes? That's at night. The sun wouldn't bother your eyes."

"The fire burns them," said Tekakwitha, glad of so ready an excuse. She had a horror of burnings and would have thought it a sin to watch her tribe's worst enemy being tortured. Not for the world, though, would she have hurt her friend's feelings by saying so.

"Four cabbage leaves for pot covers," she said, tearing off the big outer leaves, "and plenty of corn blades." She slipped them into her basket.

"I must go now, Anidas," she said, glancing up at Great Pine. "I shall get more eel skins and make you some pretty red ribbons for your hair because you helped me pound the corn."

She said good-by to her friend and went up the hill toward the village. With the sun behind her now, she could make better speed.

Arrived at the lodge, she went into the shed at the back.

"Green corn bread! Green corn bread!" She hummed happily as she went over to the woodpile and carefully selected some good dry oak barks. Green corn bread was a special delicacy. It was sweeter than the bread made of ripe dry corn, and her uncle liked it best.

After lighting the fire in the yard, she kneaded her flour into a soft dough. Then she took out the corn leaves, filled each one from a wooden ladle with some of the mixture, wrapped them up carefully, and set them side by side on the dry, hot ashes.

There was still time while the bread was baking to go for water. The shadows were nearly at their shortest as Tekakwitha came toward the lodge with her water-filled jug on her shoulder. She put it down in the shed and went over to the fire. The bread was baked to a rich golden brown. Putting the loaves into a basket, she hurried into the longhouse.

5. The Tree of Peace

HER UNCLE HAD JUST ARRIVED WITH A VISITOR, and her aunt was busily serving them food hot from the fire when Tekakwitha appeared.

Uncle Onsengongo had a vast appetite after hunting, for, like other Indians, he always hunted on an empty stomach.

"The black bear died like an old woman, not like a man or a hero," he said, gulping down a bowl of *sagamite* and handing it back for more.

Tekakwitha filled it again. As she passed it back to him she could see at a glance that the visitor was also a Mohawk chief.

"And there's a deer a little farther along the trail," continued her uncle without taking his eyes off his food. "You'll find the first sign on Hemlock Hill on the trunk of Old Man Cedar."

These directions were for the womenfolk. They would have to drag the deer back if it were not too big. But the bear they would have to cut up and bring home in pieces.

Tekakwitha looked at the visitor's bowl. He had taken only what politeness required of him and seemed no longer interested in food. He must have eaten already, she thought. Or perhaps he has too much news on his stomach. By the way her uncle avoided looking at him, she felt that big questions must be brewing. But one didn't talk about weighty matters while eating. One waited till later when the calumets were lit.

After dinner the two chiefs squatted on the mat, filled their calumets with tobacco, and lighted them with a brand from the fire.

For several moments the silence between them was unbroken. Uncle's great head looked heavier than ever, for he was trying hard not to fall asleep. His copper face glistened with oil, and his huge stomach heaved rhythmically up and down.

At last he spoke without looking up. "Tekakwitha, leave your aunt to fetch the game. You will prepare a comfortable mat for Bright Feather. He will pass the night here."

"Yes, Father," said the girl. And I shall not forget a box of bear grease for his feet, in case they are tired, she thought.

The silence broken, Bright Feather took a great puff of smoke and drew it deep into his lungs. "A black cloud has arisen down yonder in Quebec, the City of the French King," he said, eyeing the Tortoise Chief's still profile. "Great Mountain, the French war chief, is angry with us for breaking our treaty. He is ready to make war on our five Iroquois nations."

The older chief let a mouthful of smoke slowly pour from his parted lips.

"These are not just singing birds that fly by?" he asked, looking straight ahead.

Bright Feather reached for his speech bag, drew out a wampum belt of white and mauve beads with symbols on it, and handed it to the other. "The chief of the Onondagas, our father nation, sent it to me underground," he said.

At sight of this official notice, the Tortoise Chief nodded. "I have heard it," he said, passing back the belt.

"He advises that a council fire be kindled in the City of the French King and that we send ambassadors from each of our five nations to tell Great Mountain that we are ready to bury the hatchet so that the rivers will not run with blood."

Uncle Onsengongo looked sourly down the stem of his pipe. "I would rather have Great Mountain's scalp than make peace with him," he said sullenly.

"You would find this difficult, my brother, mighty chief though you are. They say that the hair on his head is as thick as a walnut bush and that it flows down over both his shoulders in waves like the sea."

"It is unfair," said the Tortoise Chief scornfully. "A brave warrior will leave only one lock so that if his enemy has courage enough and is clever enough to take it, he may."

Again there was a long silence. Through veils of smoke the Tortoise Chief's eyes smoldered with hate like burning coals.

They stick in my belly, these French, he was thinking. It's not just the size of their army; it's the strange powers!

Bright Feather seemed to read his thoughts. "They say that when their army marches it is as though a forest of trees was on the move," he said. "And there is a noise like the rumbling of thunder which they say are the voices of their demons."

The older chief's lips took a fiercer grip of his pipe. Pride was battling in him against fear. Only this very year, right in the middle of the mouse and squirrel month when the snow was thickest and the lakes were covered with ice, one of the French king's warrior chiefs, Courcelles, had brought an army right into the very heart of Iroquois country. He had been forced to retreat, but it was only the winter that beat him. Now it was high summer and there would be no snow for a long time.

"I have agreed to go myself to Quebec," continued Bright Feather. "Two warriors from my village will go with me, and we are taking a French prisoner and wampum peace belts to show that we shall keep our word. Will you send a warrior from here?"

"We shall discuss this matter tonight at a council fire with the ancients," said the Tortoise Chief. "I think we shall send Agariata."

"Agariata!" exclaimed Bright Feather, leaning forward uneasily. "Agariata was with the band of Mohawks that killed the four Frenchmen. Two of the dead men were Great Mountain's family—his brother's son and the son of his aunt."

"Does Great Mountain see so far that he knows who killed them?" asked the Tortoise Chief with a mocking smile.

Bright Feather made no answer. "Agariata is fiery," he said.

"It is well," said the other. "We shall show these fire-striking warriors of the French king that our fire is in our braves. I have spoken."

He rose stiffly from the mat. "Tekakwitha!" he called.

"Yes, Father," she said, laying down her sewing.

"Bring me the wampum belt that you have been making."

She bundled up her work and came toward him. "There it is," she said, unfolding a belt about three feet long and three inches wide. Only three or four inches of eel skin were left to be covered with beads.

"It will do for one of the peace belts," said the Tortoise Chief. "Can you finish this today?"

"Easily, Father," said the girl brightly.

The two chiefs knocked the ashes from their pipes and went toward the door. "And you will take Grandfather a bag of tobacco and tell him there will be a council fire tonight at the rising of the moon," called back her uncle.

Grandfather! thought Tekakwitha. I have been so busy lately that I have scarcely seen anything of him. I shall take my work and sit beside him while I finish it.

And I'll take him some of my bread, too, she said to herself as she pressed as much tobacco as she could into the fire bag.

Her heart warmed within her as she approached the lodge where the old man now lived.

"*Sago! Sago!*" she said, greeting the other members of the lodge as she walked through to Grandfather's mat.

He was fast asleep. Quietly she arranged herself on the mat opposite and took out her needle.

How happy she felt this afternoon. A visit with her old friend was a rare treat for her, partly because she loved him for himself and partly because he was the only one left now who brought her mother's presence close to her. Koincha and her family had gone to live at Onontagé, and Anastasia had gone away, too. She wasn't sure where.

The others who had known her mother all seemed to live just in today and for what today brought. But Grandfather lived mostly in yesterday, and last summer, and long ago. When she chatted with him, or just sat beside him, even if he slept, it was as if the broken fragments of her life came together, just as if someone had taken them like scattered beads and threaded them on one string. And though he called her Tekakwitha like the others, or Little Friend, she felt once again that she was Beautiful Day, and all the charm and sweetness of those years with her gentle mother shone round her like a calm and golden light.

Grandfather stirred restlessly. Slowly and painfully he sat up. "So it's Little Friend!" he said, rubbing the sleep from his eyes.

"I've a present for you, Grandfather, when

you're wide enough awake to see it," said Tekakwitha, handing him the tobacco and the green
corn bread. "I baked it myself—the bread, I mean.
Uncle Onsengongo sent the tobacco and told
me to tell you that there would be a council
fire tonight at the rising of the moon."

"*Agghé!*" exclaimed the old man. "I've been
dreaming that our braves were all putting on the
war paint. War with the French! War with the
French! I can feel it in my old bones. I heard
that the Bâtard Flammand arrived this morning
to see your uncle."

"Bright Feather, Grandfather."

"It's the same, Little Friend. The French called
him the Bâtard Flammand and the name's stuck."

Tekakwitha knitted her brow into a little
frown. "What kind of treaty did we make with
the French, Grandfather?" she asked. "Was it
something we should never have broken?"

"It was a peace treaty, Tekakwitha," said the
old man. "There was a time when our people
would have died rather than break a treaty, and
the ambassador of an enemy could count on
hospitality with us, even if our answer to his
people was that we would never agree to peace."

He passed his withered hand over his few
white hairs. "*Agghé!*" he sighed. "The times
have changed so since the palefaces came to our
land. It is they who have brought us the terrible
plagues like the one that hurt your eyes, Teka-

kwitha, and the firewater that drives our bravest men mad. But where was I?"

"You were telling me about treaties, Grandfather."

"Oh, yes. When I was a young man treaties were always made in some pleasant and shady grove where the little birds with their cheerful songs seemed to tune our minds to friendliness. But now when we must discuss peace with the palefaces we have no choice of the spot for a sacred council fire. It is always at one of those horrid places surrounded with mounds and ditches. The great guns on wheels gape at us with wide-open mouths, as though ready to swallow us up, so that we cannot speak from our hearts as brothers ought to do!"

"Wouldn't you like to try some of the tobacco I brought you?" Tekakwitha suggested, seeing that he looked worn and worried. War with the French seemed to matter much less to her just now than peace inside Grandfather.

The old man reached for his pipe and filled it with crooked, clumsy fingers while Tekakwitha got up to fetch him a firebrand. Even in his lodge he always offered the first puff in honor of the Master of Life, blowing it solemnly up toward the ceiling.

"Two more short rows and I shall have finished my belt," said the girl. "Tell me, how is

your rheumatism these days? Do you still go
to the sweat ovens?"

"I'm too old for it now, Tekakwitha," he
said. "It takes the sap out of an ancient tree
to sweat like that. But I was thinking today . . ."

The old man looked dreamily past her down
a long corridor of years.

"There was a little plant for the healing of
rheumatism and other sicknesses, too. I don't remember what it looked like. But this plant—and
others, too, that were for healing—they were frail
little things and touchy, for they wanted none
but the hands of a virgin to pluck them or they
lost their power to heal."

Tekakwitha had finished her work. Her dark
eyes fixed on Grandfather's were full of wonder.

"You have never told me that before," she
said. "Do the other people of our tribe know
about it, or just you?"

"It has been knowledge among our people
since the dawn of time, Little Friend," said the
old man. "But things have changed so! *Agghé*,
it's another world since the coming of the palefaces with their big guns!"

Tekakwitha unrolled her belt with its rows
and rows of glistening white and purple beads.
"This is for healing, too," she said softly.

He took the end of it playfully. "This is to
plant the tree of peace on the highest mountain.
This is to light fires of welcome in all our dwell-

ings so that all nations may trustfully come to warm themselves."

"Still young enough to make speeches, Grandfather!" laughed Tekakwitha. "You would make a splendid ambassador. They should send you to the City of the French King."

She slipped the belt and her needle into her basket and rose to go. "*Onan*, Grandfather," she said. "And try, try to remember what the little plant looks like."

It was late afternoon when she started on the homeward path. Grandfather's longhouse was close to the forest, and, by taking a little detour, she could go part of the way by a woodland trail.

The forest was alight with green and gold and filled with the scent of bracken, moss, and warm, ripe blackberries.

Suddenly she stood quite still, her head lifted as though to listen to something faint and far away. The mellow August sunlight made a soft radiance behind her, and the sweet song of a hermit thrush fell like dew into the golden cup of silence.

Will the flower of it be all white like the lily of the valley? she was wondering. Her lips parted in a little smile.

In the crook of an old oak tree a small grey squirrel, holding a nut in his two tiny paws, nibbled furiously.

At the sound of sharp teeth on shell, she looked up.

"Bright Eyes," she said gaily, "go and find Grandfather's flower."

Frightened by her voice, the squirrel stopped eating and fidgeted nervously. Then, seeing that she meant no harm, he stared back at her curiously, fascinated by the flicker of light on the glass beads of her heavy necklaces and bracelets.

A little peal of laughter made him drop his nut and scamper away up the trunk of the tree.

"And when you have found it, Little Brother," she called, "come and take me to it."

I shall pluck it for Grandfather myself, and I shall go on plucking it for him even if he lives to be as old as Great Pine on the hill, she thought, as she went on her way.

And, without knowing why, suddenly she glanced down at the blue bead on her moccasin.

6. *Drums in the Dark*

OH, WHAT A STIR THERE WAS IN THE CITY
of Quebec this bright September morning in
1666! The great day had arrived for the French
army to leave for the campaign against the Iroquois, and the soldiers of the king were parading
in front of the governor's palace.

The very earth and the buildings seemed to
rock and sway to the stirring rhythm of marching
feet, the roll of the drums, and the blare of silver

bugles that cried the glory of France into the clear, golden air.

Children clung to the long, billowing skirts of their mothers or perched on strong shoulders, watching with wonder and excitement while the troops marched up and down before their eyes.

"That's the Carignan regiment from France," cried a small boy as 600 soldiers of the best and bravest in Europe, all in spotless white uniforms with black velvet trimmings, black leggings, and black tricorn hats with silver braid, marched proudly by.

After them came the 600 French-Canadians wearing whatever battle dress they could find in Canada for the event, and, in the rear, marched 100 half-naked Hurons and Algonquins, looking a little self-conscious but feeling vastly secure at being attached to so mighty an army.

A little aloof stood the high officers, Governor Courcelles among them, keen as a battle blade and itching, as usual, to be off.

Suddenly a great cheer went up from the crowd as the Marquis of Tracy, lieutenant general of the king's armies, he whom the savages called Great Mountain, came out of the governor's palace. He walked onto the parade ground, flashing with splendor in his scarlet coat embroidered with silver, white stockings and tricorn hat with its waving white ostrich plumes. Everything about him was huge—the massive head with its flowing black wig, the long, heavy nose, and the square, high shoulders that outtopped all the other officers.

"Where are all those soldiers going, Mummy?" asked a small girl. Her mother's tears were flowing so fast that she made no reply. For her the entire Carignan regiment was not equal in splendor to one French-Canadian soldier in an old faded blue suit.

"Don't you know?" piped up a six-year-old soldier in the bud. "They're going down to the place where those Iroquois martyred Father Jogues and René Goupil."

"Look at that!" cried another little boy indignantly. "There's an Indian over there on the officers' side. He has a much better view than we have!"

It was Bright Feather, known by the French as the Bâtard Flammand. The marquis had given him a special place from which to watch so that this chief of the proud-stepping Iroquois tribe, who had terrorized New France for the past twenty years, should believe and tremble at the sight of the French army.

Deafened by the rolling of the drums, Bright Feather would have given all his furs for the past ten years to have been back in the peace and quiet of his own native village.

It turned one's bones to wax and one's heart to water to see the splendor and might of the soldiers of the king, and it humiliated him to the very dust to see the Algonquins and Hurons marching behind them holding their heads like conquerors. And now, to shame him still further, he realized that he was weeping just like any squaw, the tears pouring down his cheeks and dropping to the ground.

And it's all Agariata's fault, he thought bitterly. Everything had been going well for the peace. Great Mountain had invited all the ambassadors to a big feast at his own table. And it was there that all went wrong. Who was it who had begun to talk of the murder of Great Mountain's nephew? Try as he would, he could never remember, for the scene that followed had blotted everything else from his memory. He could see him now, Agariata, the fiery one, raising his right arm and crying, "This was the hand that cut off his head!"

"You'll never cut off another!" Great Mountain had thundered, rising from his seat.

That had ended the peace. Agariata had been taken out and shot before the eyes of all the ambassadors.

The Tortoise Chief had been wrong, thought Bright Feather wretchedly.

"Bâtard Flammand!" said a grave, deep voice beside him suddenly, and he looked up to see Great Mountain.

Standing there in his scanty clothing, with his

one thin scalp lock, the Mohawk chief felt like a skinned rabbit up against a huge grizzly bear.

"You see the army we are taking to your country?" said Great Mountain. "What have you to say?"

"Ononthio," said the Iroquois, summoning up all his remaining courage, "it is clear to me that we are lost, but our loss will cost you dearly. Our nation will be wiped out, but I warn you that many of your fine young men will perish, for my people will defend themselves to the very end. Only one thing I do beg you. Save my wife and my children at Onneyout."

The sixty-four-year-old soldier looked steadily down at the Mohawk chief. Duties to God and the king had planted a deep frown on his forehead between his eyes, and a great furrow ran down both cheeks, but there was no cruelty in his face. Iroquois as a tribe might be a hive of bees to be burnt out, but there was something pitiful about one single Iroquois pleading with tears for his wife and children, and the man had spoken with courage.

"I give my promise that we shall do our best to save them all, and we shall bring them back to you here," he said.

When they looked back at the army it was moving briskly down toward the St. Lawrence River, the crowd following and cheering.

A wild peal of bells began to ring out from all

the four churches of Quebec, and a salvo of guns thundered a savage salute from the palace terrace.

At the foot of the hill, the fleet was waiting. The Marquis of Tracy, Courcelles, and four priests were the first to enter the boats. The other officers and soldiers followed.

Hands were clasped in farewell. Women wept silently and children cried aloud to be taken.

When the boats were all full, another salvo of guns shook the town.

Swiftly the fleet moved up the river, past the ramparts, past the high, tree-crowned cliffs, until it rounded the point at Sillery and was lost to view.

Two hundred and fifty miles down in Iroquois country summer had gone. The sunflowers bowed down their sleepy heads while Indians picked the tightly packed seeds from them and pounded them into rich brown oil. The Bâtard Flammand had been gone nearly two moons and still no news had come from him.

And time passed by, turning on autumn's glowing, golden wheel. In the hot silence of mid-September woods, boughs were bent down under their heavy burden of fruit, and the chestnuts were ready to fall to the earth for ripeness. A pair of brown hands, clearer and finer in texture than the hands of any white girl, moved quickly among the leaves of the crabapple tree, plucking the rosy apples and placing them in corn-husk baskets. They were the hands of Tekakwitha. I wonder where my peace belt is now, she was thinking. Will it be sparkling in the hair of the French chief, Great Mountain?

The fields belonging to the women sprawled comfortably beneath the cloudless blue sky. Folded in their green, bearded sheaths, the corn-cobs slowly changed from white to gold. Shall we gather in the harvest, wondered the squaws? Will there be peace or war?

Mothers with new-born babies and mothers expecting babies never neglected to fling an extra big offering of fat into the fire to the Master of Life before every meal. "Let it be peace," their hearts were saying. "Let us have our children in safety."

Now and again passing travelers brought news. "They say that the peace is broken and that Great Mountain is coming himself. They say . . ." But to all such rumors the Tortoise Chief merely shook his head. "I have not heard it," he said. His face with its deep creases was like a false face frozen into a sour grimace, but his heart was heavy with foreboding as a cloud is heavy with rain.

During the last days of September, the 1300 soldiers from Quebec, with their officers and 110 volunteers from Montreal, met together at Fort St. Anne on Lake Champlain in the midst of a forest of beautiful pine trees.

From Lake Champlain to Lake Blessed Sacrament they had to make a difficult portage through bush, carrying supplies and canoes. But this was nothing to the trials that lay ahead.

Slowly and painfully, loaded with baggage and food packs, the soldiers began to cross the hundred miles of forest trail and mountain that lay between them and the Mohawks. In endless, uneven files they moved along, falling over stumps and roots, sinking into deep mud, slithering down ravines and clambering up rocky slopes.

September passed by, and the October forests flamed with gold and scarlet. Still the army plodded on, sleeping at night on the muddy soil or on beds of damp leaves.

Up at Gandawagué Tekakwitha was squatted on her mat in the lodge, sewing a new cloak for her uncle.

Suddenly he entered hastily with a wampum belt in one hand and a dead turkey in the other. Tekakwitha rose instantly, sensing a crisis.

He held out the bird to her and flung the belt on his mat.

"Prepare the stockade," he said tersely, as he tore off his leggings and upper tunic. "The French are coming."

Tekakwitha rushed for the shed, seized a bucket of water, and headed for the stockade. Already women, young and old, were swarming up the notched log ladders, carrying buckets, jugs, and bark pails of water to the fighting platform at the top.

It was hard and dangerous climbing for her frail body. Her head ached with the effort, and her stomach, always easily upset, grew queasy as she mounted higher and higher. Half-blinded, she bowed her head to the wall, almost closing her eyes against the sharp October sunlight that glinted like spears through the partly stripped trees.

For hours the squaws worked this way, lines of women going to the well for more water until every last container stood on the stockade as a protection against fire.

Darkness fell. Men with guns and bows waited and watched on the fighting platform and women slept fitfully. When dawn broke, the first refugees from other villages began to stream into Gandawagué.

Before sunset a spy brought news. Three villages had already been taken. Terrified by the noise of the drum devils and the sight of so huge an army, the Mohawks had fled before a shot had been fired. There remained only two more villages, and one of these was Gandawagué, the strongest of them all—Gandawagué, with its high triple stockade and the four bastions at each corner. Would the enemy come in the night or would they wait for dawn?

But the French army would not wait till dawn.

Slowly, from tree to tree, the soldiers advanced, while all the time the drums kept throbbing and throbbing, beating a hollow tattoo for the plodding of weary feet.

Now and then Iroquois spies brought news of the army's approach. "They are more numerous than the leaves on a tree," they said.

It was almost midnight before the drums could be heard from the village. Dogs moved uneasily at the sound, the hair bristling on their backs. Then one of them threw back its head and howled mournfully at the moon.

Nearer and nearer came the army, and louder and louder grew the sound of the drums, more maddening and mysterious at every minute. As the first shadowy figures began to appear on the edge of the forest, a cloud covered the moon. Under a cloak of thick darkness the French soldiers began to climb the hill to Gandawagué. As they did so, from every drum came a mighty, ear-splitting crash and then a long, hoarse growl like a band of wild beasts bent on destruction.

To the Mohawks crouched on the fighting platform, it seemed as though all hell had been let loose. There was a moment of hesitation charged with panic. Then the Tortoise Chief sprang to his feet. "To the forest, Brothers!" he shouted. "Everyone is against us!" Taking the lead, he fairly leaped from the stockade.

A wild stampede followed. Buckets were

knocked over; dogs barked in frenzy; children, snatched from their mats, screamed with terror. In the darkness people were kicked and bowled over in the dust.

Tekakwitha and her aunt were at the door of the lodge when the Tortoise Chief reached them. "A *happis!*" he cried to Tekakwitha. She ran to fetch a burden strap. Hastily he tied one end around his right wrist and the other around her left. A short-sighted girl could stumble and get lost in the dark.

For several minutes the whole village ran helter-skelter. Indians rushed through the doors of the stockade and dashed for the forest as though the drum devils were at their very heels.

When the French army entered the village, there was complete silence. In the midst of the deserted compound, dazed but stubborn, stood two old squaws who had refused to leave the place.

All that night the French soldiers slept soundly on Iroquois mats. In the morning one other human being was found—a very old man who had hidden under a canoe. He was stiff and in extreme pain from exposure and damp. "*Agghé!*" was all he said as they helped him to his feet.

Grandfather's mind was wandering and his teeth chattering as he sat on an overturned bucket watching the French soldiers fall into rank in front of the village. I'm so old now that I'm the only one left of all my world, he thought.

A big wooden cross was planted in front of the doors of the stockade and a post was erected bearing the arms of the French king. Then a Mass of thanksgiving was said to the God of armies. Voices rose in the *Te Deum*.

Then the French soldiers set fire to all the standing crops and to all the buildings in Gandawagué.

"We will give you your freedom," they told Grandfather and the two old squaws. With great difficulty the old man hobbled off in the direction of the forest. But the two old women, seeing the fire burning their homes and their fields, threw themselves into the flames.

Four hundred Mohawks died of cold and famine that winter, for it was too late in the year to build new lodges and there was not nearly enough food for three thousand homeless Indians.

One day, when the snow was still on the ground, Bright Feather came back with a message from Great Mountain himself: "I give you Iroquois four moons to send hostages and peace ambassadors. If you fail to do so, I shall return myself to your country at the head of my troops, and this time you will not get off so easily."

It took six moons and still another threat from the marquis before the stubborn Mohawk nation obeyed. Another peace treaty was drawn up in

Quebec. The Iroquois solemnly signed it with the pictures of their totems: Wolf, Bear, Tortoise. "Send blackrobes to live with us," they said, not because they wanted to become Christians, but because blackrobes were French treasure and would make good hostages.

It was agreed. Missionaries would go to Mohawk country the following year.

And so, at long last, Grandfather's tree of peace was planted and was to stay alive in New France for eighteen years. But Tekakwitha's old friend was never to see it, for another kind of tree gave all its dead leaves to cover up his body when he fell from exhaustion and fever alone in the forest.

7. Living Water

THOUGH SHE WAS RIGHT INSIDE THE LONG-
house, busying herself about the fire and food
pots, Tekakwitha heard the hullabaloo away off
down by the river—the frenzied fanfare of shell
trumpets, the frantic yells and hoots of the Iroquois.

The canoes must be arriving, she thought, as a
little tremor of expectation, all mixed with shyness and eagerness, ran through her veins. The

people of the village were welcoming the three blackrobes who were coming to stay a few days in the lodge of the Tortoise Chief, and Uncle Onsengongo had given Tekakwitha entire charge of looking after their needs.

She cast a quick glance around the lodge. Everything was in readiness now. There was plenty of food, all hot and ready to serve. The three mats were comfortably laid out with a thought for extra warmth, for Aunt Teedah had told her that the French did not wear the skins of animals. They will feel at home under those covers, she thought, as she looked with satisfaction at the new, bright red blankets her uncle had traded with the broadbreeches at Fort Albany.

Satisfied that nothing had been forgotten, she went to the door of the lodge. Not even a hound was in sight. She slipped down to the gate of the stockade.

Down below the waving green corn was Old Friend Mohawk River. Only now she was looking at him from another direction, for the new village of Kanawaki had crossed the water and the lodges were huddled on a high hill a few miles up the river.

It sounds like the noise they made when my father came home in triumph, thought Tekakwitha, as another wild outburst of cheering reached her ears.

She could not make out the canoes or the

crowd. Nor did she strain her eyes to try to see, for she was not curious. She had wanted only to get closer to the rejoicing, and now it set little flutes piping all up and down her heart. The French were my mother's friends, she was telling herself.

How the trumpets blared and tooted! How the Iroquois roared and laughed, danced and sang! This was their way of telling the French peacemakers that they wanted to be their friends as long as the sun shone and the rivers ran with water. For the joy in them was joy for the keeping of their crops, and the laughter in them was laughter for the safety of their children and the sureness of their lodges.

Aunt Teedah would be down there among the crowd, but Uncle Onsengongo was not there. He was away with a party of warriors fighting the Indians of the Wolf nation. The hated French blackrobes were not coming at any invitation of his.

A little guilty feeling crept into Tekakwitha's heart at the thought of Uncle Onsengongo. He would be angry with me if he knew how glad I am, she thought. He had been very gruff and hostile with her for the past two moons, ever since Aunt Teedah had nagged her again about getting married and Tekakwitha had pleaded that she was too young and had asked for more time to think about it. It hurt her, not just because Uncle Onsengongo was cold and hard, but because she really owed him something for taking care of her and couldn't pay him back in the way he wished.

But I'll make it up to him by working very hard, she thought. And I shall look after . . .

A sudden panic seized her as she realized that the voices were much nearer now and the crowd was surging up the hill. At that moment so great a shyness overwhelmed her that she would have given all she had to have taken to her heels and scampered off like a little rabbit into the forest. Instead of that, she ran back to the longhouse. She must never betray the trust that her uncle had put in her. Hate the French though he did, the peace was all wrapped up in this visit, and Iroquois hospitality must be without fault.

She heard the babel of voices filling the courtyard as the entire village, bursting with curiosity and full of high spirits, streamed through the doors of the stockade.

I've never seen a paleface before, she thought with misgiving as she drew her shawl timidly across her face.

"A princess should wear her shawl over her shoulders like other girls, not in front of her face." Long ago Uncle Onsengongo had said that to her, and here, inside the lodge, there was no excuse. Dutifully she draped it over her shoulders and stood waiting, every inch a chief's daughter, the red shawl giving a glowing touch of color to her handsome leather tunic and skirt.

She heard Aunt Teedah's sharp voice, and then three figures dressed in long black gowns and black hats as broad as cabbage leaves stepped quietly into the lodge.

"*Sago!*" said Father Frémin, Father Bruyas and Father Pierron, taking off their hats.

"*Sago*," said Tekakwitha, and the eyes that met hers were so kind and so full of gentle friendliness that all her fear and awkwardness instantly melted away.

With simple dignity she showed them their mats and then set to work serving them food. *Sagamite* came first. She had used the bowls and ladles kept for ambassadors.

There was a moment of silence as the three blackrobes bowed their heads. "*Benedicite . . .*" murmured Father Frémin in a strange tongue, and then all three crossed themselves.

Tekakwitha watched fascinated. Something sweet and familiar stirred in her breast. Deep down in the quiet pools of her mind images were forming like the pictures of cloud and blossom in the water at the spring. She saw corn, gold on the cob, and a woman's dark head bending over it. She saw a flying bird, a sunset, a dear, smiling face. Someone she had loved and lost long ago was coming back to her. A woman's arms enfolded her. Mother! thought Tekakwitha, Mother!

Food! Aunt Teedah's prod was telling her. Quickly she came back to earth. There were still the broiled sturgeon and vegetables to be served, and a basket of squash for dessert.

In little, curious groups the Iroquois trooped into the lodge to observe the foreign visitors and stood watching their every movement. They were plainly delighted to find these Frenchmen so docile and friendly compared with the wild warriors who had burned their village and all their crops just a year ago.

Aunt Teedah was getting on well with the strangers, too, and was putting out every effort to please them. Suddenly she broke off in the middle of a sentence, and a silence fell on the people as the Tortoise Chief appeared in the doorway. He was wearing his finest crest of eagle's feathers, and Tekakwitha thought she had never seen him looking so fierce and powerful.

Coldly he approached the three blackrobes who rose to meet him. He greeted them formally, shaking hands as he had seen the broadbreeches do. In eloquent language, practiced from many council meetings, he thanked the Master of Life for bringing them safely to Kanawaki.

"The Wolves should be driven off in a few days," he added, just to remind them that the credit for their safety was not all due to the Master of Life but to the Iroquois whom the French had treated so badly. "Did you hear the groans in the courtyard just now?" he asked. "That was an Iroquois squaw. She has been scalped by the Wolves just outside of this village."

"Poor woman!" exclaimed Father Frémin, touched with pity. "We shall go to visit her."

He pushed aside his empty bowl and reached for his bag. Tekakwitha watched him as he took things out and laid them on the mat—papers, a small vial of water, holy pictures. A black crucifix! Eagerly she fixed her eyes on it. She would have liked to touch it, to take it in her hands, and at the same time she felt as though something as cruel and cold as ice were restraining her. She glanced up at Uncle Onsengongo. He, too, had seen the crucifix. His eyes were narrowed on it with hate and the desire to destroy. And, as though his thoughts were as clear to her as a picture, she knew that he was remembering the big wooden cross planted by Great Mountain in front of the village of Gandawagué, standing there as he had seen it, in the midst of blackened fields and smoking cinders.

Father Frémin put the crucifix, with the water and pictures, into a small case. Then he and the other two blackrobes thanked Aunt Teedah and Tekakwitha for the good meal they had prepared, and went out.

Like squaws, thought the Tortoise Chief scornfully. And they will turn our braves into squaws, too, with their Christian gospel of peace.

Tekakwitha looked wistfully after them. Dearly would she have loved to follow them. How she would have hung on their wise words! Instead, she must be as busy as a bee in summer. But although she remained in the lodge, it was no longer the same. Now it was a tabernacle for her gentle visitors, and their presence lingered on with her as the green scent of the living forest lingered on in the new fresh wood.

All her tasks that day had a sunrise touch to them, especially if they were for her guests. She sang to herself as she baked the bread, and the birds sang with her as she went to the gardens, and the kettle hummed a cosy little tune on the fire. They look thin, she told herself. Perhaps they are half-starved and their stomachs hurt as ours did last winter in the famine.

It was dark when the priests returned to the lodge. After the meal that Tekakwitha served them, they said their evening prayers.

From a shadowy corner of the lodge Tekakwitha quietly observed her visitors, as much aware of the holiness in them as a child is aware of the perfume of a flower. How she would have liked to go to them and say, "My mother was a Christian, too," but Uncle Onsengongo would have been very displeased. Like a thirsty plant she drank in the pure water of life, without any words, absorbing it into every fiber of her being.

That night, lying awake in the dark, Teka-kwitha tried out an awkward little Sign of the Cross. That must be the Christians' totem, she thought. I am sure my mother made that sign on me with her finger before she put me to bed.

For the three days of the blackrobes' visit, the lodge of the Tortoise Chief was the village curiosity. Some visitors came bubbling with news. Among these was Tekakwitha's cousin, Katentas. She followed Tekakwitha around, telling her all she had seen of the blackrobes' doings. She told how they had visited many sick people, among them the scalped woman, how she had refused to listen to them at first, how an old woman in her lodge had chased the French out, and how, on their third visit, the dying woman had listened eagerly to their words and had become so peaceful and happy. "She is going to have the saving waters, Tekakwitha. Can't you come?"

"I have too much to do," said Tekakwitha, thinking of Uncle Onsengongo.

"Oh, I wish I had courage like Karitha!" said her cousin eagerly. "You know her—the one they say is the happiest married woman in our village. She actually went into the lodge with all our Huron Christian slaves to hear the black-robe teaching and to pray with them. She wants so much to have the saving waters that she does not mind the scoffing."

Tekakwitha said little, but in her heart she pondered over all she heard. This is my world, she thought. For it was as though she were coming home, finding something she had always half guessed at—a world of gentleness and mercy, of purity and healing.

On the fourth day the blackrobes left. "What a modest, sweet child the little girl is," remarked Father Pierron.

"She behaves just like a well-brought-up French girl," said Father Frémin. "Strange and sad it is to see her with such a father."

Harvest Festival came and went, full of song and gaiety. Autumn moons, tawny and swollen, floated above the flaming forests, and pale, cold moons heralded the snow. The Winter God began his fierce battle with the Life God or the Holder of the Heavens. No longer could Tekakwitha smell the scent of the wild woods in the lodge, for it was lost in the stench of stale fish, and bear grease, and the reek of smoke that choked her lungs and scalded her eyes.

Came the shortest day of the year and, on the fifth day of the second moon after it, the New Year Festival began with its magical rites to restore the powers of the Life God. One night all the fires were put out in all the longhouses in Kanawaki. Old men came and passed from lodge to lodge, moving like ghosts down their long, dark corridors, lighting new fires in every hearth bowl. Already rumors of spring stirred in the hearts of the hopeful.

Then, from their newly lighted homes, the Iroquois streamed out to the big council meeting for thanksgiving. In the huge lodge they squatted on the ground, facing north, south, east, or west.

Aunt Teedah was anything but thankful tonight, and the voice of the Tortoise Chief uplifted in the prayers only put a sharp edge on her bitterness: "Thanks to the Master of Life for our Mother, the Earth!"

She, Teedah, had never been a mother, and now the girl she had brought up as her child had no interest in marriage at all. As a rule, all one had to do was to breathe the name of a fine brave and any natural girl would jump at the prospect. Something was wrong with Tekakwitha; it must be the Algonquin blood in her. She would send her to the woods with a wise woman to have her dreams studied.

"Thanks to the Master of Life for the grass, for the fruit of the trees . . ." droned the Tortoise Chief.

There's been no fruit in my life, thought Aunt Teedah, and now I'm getting old. Before long I'll be doing nothing but sit all day on a mat making a feather blanket like the toothless, tottering squaws. And who will bring us food if Tekakwitha doesn't marry? Ah, but it's bitter to grow old like that, bitter as the rind on an early pumpkin!

By the time the meeting was over Aunt Teedah had developed as many bristles on her soul as a porcupine has quills on its body. She had also developed a plan.

Going home under the brilliant stars, with Tekakwitha walking meekly at her side, her body was rigid with purpose under its soft furs and there was a small triumph in her heart. She had joined forces with the Master of Life himself. Tekakwitha would be married, and before the Dream Festival.

All through the days of the fire ceremonies held to drive away disease and death, Aunt Teedah plotted for life—for lives which would spring from Tekakwitha in her children.

The plan of attack began with a new dress. "It is beautiful, Aunt Teedah!" exclaimed Tekakwitha, touched by her aunt's sudden warmth.

"You will wear it tonight at the Dream Festival," said her aunt. "You are growing up into a fine young woman, Tekakwitha, and a chief's daughter should be better dressed than other girls."

Tekakwitha did her best to keep wearing a pleased look, but in her heart all her enthusiasm for the dress had vanished. Much as she loved beautiful things, it increased her shyness to appear among all the people better dressed than the others.

She was glad when the subject turned to more practical things.

"We have finished all the *sagamite*," said Aunt Teedah. "Make some more, Tekakwitha. And you will put these in it," she added, bringing her a basket of hickory nuts. Hickory nuts, especially at this time of year, were a special delicacy and used for feasts.

Someone very important must be coming to-night, thought the girl, as she set about the task of pounding the nuts in a block mortar.

"Put on your new dress now," said her aunt when the *sagamite* was finished. "I want to see how it fits."

Obediently Tekakwitha put on the rich, glossy fur robe. It was of white tanned buffalo, the kind they got only by trading with the Indians in Canada.

Then Aunt Teedah greased and combed Tekakwitha's hair till it glistened like a raven's wing, and loaded her neck and arms with new necklaces and beaded ornaments.

No sooner had she been released from her aunt's primping than a young brave whom she had never seen before entered the lodge with Uncle Onsengongo. He was tall and very handsome and had two splendid silver fox pelts over one shoulder.

Victory gleamed in Aunt Teedah's eyes as she greeted him. Tekakwitha pretended not to see the stranger. She squatted on her mat and busied herself with a basket of sewing.

"A present!" said the young brave loudly, tossing the soft pelts over a rafter. Eagerly he looked at Tekakwitha. Then, striding quickly over to her mat, he squatted down beside her, staring at her with admiring eyes.

Burning from head to foot with misery and embarrassment, the girl rose quickly as though to fetch something outside. But Aunt Teedah had seen her move and stood in her way. She had a bowl of *sagamite* in her hands. "Our daughter made this specially for you," she said to the young man, "and wants to give it to you her-self."

Surprised and confused, Tekakwitha hesitated a moment like a trapped animal. The blood pounded in her throat, her temples. Then, like a flash, she understood the trick and her aunt's part in it—the new dress, the special *sagamite*. . . . A gift of food to a man was a promise of marriage.

Something she had never felt before in all her life rose inside her—hot anger, indignation, and a fixed determination not to give in. A terrible courage seized her and, before anyone could stop her, she brushed past her aunt and uncle and rushed out of the door. For a second she paused there. "I shall never enter this lodge again," she cried, "until that man has gone out of it!"

Blindly she fled through the darkness. Twice she tripped and fell headlong but, not heeding her bruises and cuts, she picked herself up and ran on. Then, suddenly feeling sick and out of breath, she crept behind a big tree trunk. Leaning against it, she sobbed as though her heart would break. A dog that had followed her crept close to her body, licking her leggings and bare arms and whining in sympathy.

Tears brought relief. She felt an emptiness that was almost like peace, and then she realized that she was very cold. She turned the new dress fur inside for warmth, brushed the snow off a low stump and sat down, putting her arms around the dog's neck and laying her cheek against its head.

For a long time she remained thus. Then from far away she heard voices singing. The Dream Festival had begun. For three days the Iroquois would sing all their special songs to bring back the magical power of their personal guardian spirits. Wistful and sad the voices sounded, drifting through the darkness over the snow, singing the songs she had known ever since she was a child.

How she wished she could run back through the years, run back to her childhood and escape. But there was no turning back. You had to grow

up. It was like being caught in a rapid in a
canoe. You had to battle through!

And there's nothing I can change, she said
to herself. An apple seed can't become a pumpkin, nor a squash a bean. And this thing in her
that made her different from others had been
put in her by the Creator of all things. She could
explain it to no one, not even to herself. She
did not have to explain it to herself. It was there,
something to accept, a sacred trust that she must
keep, that she *would* keep, though she would be
soft and yielding in everything else.

I'll work my fingers to skin and bone for Uncle
Onsengongo and Aunt Teedah, she thought, for
I've never wanted to hurt anything or anybody.
Never, never!

She got up and walked slowly back to the
lodge, peering inside first to be sure it was empty.
The wood supply by the fire was almost done.
She went to the shed and fetched more, setting
it down tidily by the hearth.

It will be colder tonight, she said to herself
and laid an extra blanket down on Uncle Onsengongo's and Aunt Teedah's mat.

Satisfied that there was enough food on the
fire for them in case they came in hungry, she
went to bed.

When she got up the next morning it was to
be treated not as a daughter but as a slave, as
the poorest slave. All the ugliest tasks were for

her. Sweetly and patiently she did them all. There were no more kind words for her, only harshness and a coldness that she had never known before. But there was a smile on her face, and in her breast a song that only the pure in heart and the humble in spirit can know.

8. Saving Waters

THE REEDS AND GRASSES WHISPERED AND gossiped in the breeze as Tekakwitha, barefooted and barelegged, waded in the pond among the water lilies.

What a sight the lilies were! The yellow ones —all yellow, each with its little image in the water, wavering and flickering like the priest's candles she had once seen when she had peeped inside the door of the new chapel. And the white ones! As though some clever hand had carved them out of snow and then put a bit of sunlight in the center for a golden heart!

As she bent down to pluck a white one, she paused a moment, feasting her eyes on its loveliness. Three drops of water, radiant with light, lay cradled in its pure white petals. "Little baptized one," she murmured, "you, too, have your roots in the slime, and alas, my people like them for food, Uncle Onsengongo especially."

Reluctantly she pried at the root until it came away with a soft sucking sound. A little sigh escaped her lips as she put it into her basket with the others. How long was it since the first blackrobes had come? Nearly three autumns! And now they had Father Frémin all the time, and a chapel. And still I am not . . .

What was that? Suddenly she stood very still and her heart leaped with fear as the sharp staccato sound of a rattle reached her ears. Never had she heard that sound since her father's death without a feeling of terror.

Dropping her basket of lilies, she ducked down behind a clump of bushes. For a few seconds all she could hear was the wild pounding of her heart and the throaty complaint of a frog. Then it came again. Rattle, rattle, rattle! She could hear loud, rough voices and the occasional tap of a stick on a wooden water drum.

Peering between the branches she could see

three figures coming toward the pond. They've been drinking firewater, she thought desperately, as she watched their faltering steps. Cautiously she wriggled further and further into the bushes. Here she would wait until they had gone by.

But, to her horror, they did not pass by. They came around the pool and began to walk in her direction. Would they discover her basket and then look for her? How she shrank from the evil that was in these men! They were so near now that she could see them clearly. All three were members of the secret society of False Face Healers. She could tell that by their hideous wooden masks and their hair that hung down in front over their shoulders in thin, snaky coils.

They were within a stone's throw of her hide-out when the Crooked-mouth Doctor slumped down on the bank and, shoving up his mask, raised an elk bladder flask to his lips. The other two dropped down beside him and did the same.

For a few minutes they all sat silently drinking. "To the devil with the blackrobe!" said a voice behind the Spoon-lipped Doorkeeper mask. His false face wore the expression of an unhappy old man, but his voice was full of fire and energy. As he spoke, he shook his head so violently that the three little sacks of sacred tobacco tied near the part of his hair bobbed up and down.

"I would kill him with my own hands if it

were not for the peace!" This time it was the voice behind the Whistling Beggar mask that spoke. It was harsh and wicked and went oddly with the foolish, innocent expression of his false face—the round, owlish eyes, and the tiny round hole of a mouth surrounded by rays, as though forever pursed up to whistle.

The Crooked-mouth Doctor said nothing. He merely shook his rattle and turned his face with the twisted grin—the nose like a battered pumpkin stalk, and the sad, crescent-moon eyes—in the direction of the speaker.

"We'll all be out of business one day if this French blackrobe stays much longer," continued the Whistling Beggar. "Who will make us strong with presents if more people join the praying Christians?"

"Who indeed!" said the Spoon-lipped Door-keeper with the pained, anxious eyes. "And the other jugglers—the old men that bring the rain and make the love potions—they are faring no better. Chenos brought down rain in Gandagaro when the corn was drying on its stalks. The women made him strong with wampum beads and tobacco, but the blackrobe told the people later, 'It is not Chenos who brings the rain but the Master of Life. Chenos just reads His message in the waters and the skies as you read the symbols on your wampum belts.'"

The Whistling Beggar gave a little impatient

tap on his water drum. "What chance have we to work out healings with our ceremonies and our feasts when these Christians take pleasure only in what they call the cross? There is no frightening them any more, not even the squaws, and they are usually the best clients."

The Crooked-mouth Doctor raised himself on one elbow and began to talk in a voice that sounded to Tekakwitha strangely small and cowardly compared with his huge, bold mask.

"I'm for the English and the Dutch!" he exclaimed. "They give us brandy and guns and help us get the furs from the Algonquins and Hurons, but the French! Bah! Their great chiefs forbid them to give us firewater, and they train our enemies to fight against us. Then they come with their ceremonies and their feasts and talk about love and the cross until the hearts melt in our bravest men, and they bury their hatchets and some even let themselves be burned and die singing their hymns and calling out that they forgive their enemies. Squaws, I tell you, the lot of them! Bah!"

Fiercely he drained his flask and rose unsteadily to his feet. The others followed. With boundless relief Tekakwitha watched them go, but she did not move from her hiding place until the last sound of their voices had died away.

Hastily she filled her basket. Not until she

reached the village did she feel safe. At the sight of a group of Indians gathered under a large oak tree, listening to the blackrobe, she paused and squatted behind them. Here in the pure, sweet air of the Christian faith she would shake off the foul breath of evil that she felt in the presence of the jugglers.

She would not have time to listen to a sermon, but it took only a few moments to refresh her soul with thoughts of goodness and heaven, for Father Frémin had painted some of the great Christian truths on canvas in pictures and symbols. There were the seven sacraments, the three great virtues of faith, hope, and charity, all the commandments of God, and heaven and hell. With her quick, intelligent mind, she had soon understood and felt all this in her own way. Sometimes Father Frémin would leave his pictures pinned to trees for a few days. Then she would come all alone, between the busy tasks of the day, and stand gazing at them, lost in ecstasy.

Now this morning the voices of the people broke in on her meditations.

"Do they eat moose and deer in heaven?" asked an old warrior. "And do they kill men and take their scalps? Without these things I will not believe."

"If you desire these things in heaven, you will have them," said Father Frémin patiently.

At this there was a roar of laughter, for the

blackrobe had made a mistake in the Iroquois language.

How tired he looks, thought Tekakwitha, and he teaches my people all for love. How I wish I could give him my lilies for his chapel.

"Do the Algonquins and Hurons go to heaven, too?" asked another.

"If they are good, they go there," said Father Frémin.

"Then I prefer not to go at all," said the questioner.

"Nor will you," said Father Frémin, "if you go on offending the loving God by your sins. And hell . . ." He pointed to the picture of hell and began to give a vivid description of it.

This was too much for one of the old squaws. She put a fat finger in each ear so as not to hear. Several old men and women followed her example. But Father Frémin was equal to that trick. He drew another picture of an old woman stopping her ears while demons threw hot coals into them.

There was an uncomfortable murmur of surprise and horror. Down came the hands from all the ears, and a quiet respect settled on the group.

As Tekakwitha picked up her basket to go, she looked down at one of the white blossoms. I shall keep my soul as pure as that for the Great Master of Life and Love, she told herself.

At the lodge Aunt Teedah took the lilies from her to prepare the roots for the pot. More and more she was leaving Tekakwitha free to make the beautiful things that only she could do to perfection.

And how joyously the girl took to this artistic work! Often the lazy Iroquois girls would drop in to watch with envy and admiration while she made a fire bag, a pair of hunter's moccasins, or a baby's cradle, decorating them with clever designs of her own creation in beads, porcupine quills, and shells which she had dyed herself in all the colors of the rainbow.

Aunt Teedah had long since ceased to treat her as a slave. Her unfailing sweetness and her willing, gentle spirit had melted the ice on her aunt's heart. Even Uncle Onsengongo had come to accept her as she was. She was useful to him, and he could find no fault in her except her interest in Christianity. It had not escaped his eagle eyes, but he put it down to a girl's whim. Squaws, he would say to himself—they run after any newfangled thing that these palefaces bring them. One day it's a silver brooch or a shawl; the next it's the cross. As for him, he hated this Christian gospel, and if he let it go on under his nose it was only because he thought of it as an unhealthy fungus growing on the tree of peace. One had to take the one with the other.

Time passed by and after three years, Father

Frémin left and Father Boniface took his place—
Father Boniface, with his love for music, who
trained small Iroquois seven and eight years old
to sing so sweetly that their pure voices in the
chapel became one of the village attractions.

But it was at Christmas time that Father Boniface gave the people of Kanawaki the greatest
surprise. In a corner of the little bark chapel, all
decorated with evergreens and twinkling candles,
he had set up the manger of Bethlehem. All that
day he remained beside it, telling and retelling
the wonderful story. Out of the snow the Indians trooped in to listen and gaze with awe and
curiosity at the scene—the humble lodge with
Sose and the Virgin Wari and a beautiful little
papoose, Iesos, sleeping on the moss, while angels
looked down with wonder from the rafters and
shepherds came with their sheep to visit.

The Iroquois were enchanted. Even many
pagans came to church that day. Aunt Teedah
was there, pleased and puzzled and a little en-
vious of the Mother of Iesos. The Master of Life,
a little Baby born of a Virgin! That—now that
turned all her careful calculations upside down.
But gradually the hard lines and sharp angles of
her thin face relaxed. Perhaps it is natural after
all, she thought, that a little Child should be the
center of the universe.

And Tekakwitha! With what joy she listened
to the Christmas story, listened as to an old,

sweet song that she had heard once long, long
ago, whose tune she had never lost but whose
words she could not remember. And was this not
the song of her heart? Ah! what a model for
her, this pure and holy Virgin Wari, who for
love kept her body as a clean, new lodge for the
presence of the Master of Life. And did the
people of her tribe drink firewater, and do shame-
ful and cruel things, so that she sometimes covered her eyes with her shawl as Tekakwitha
covered hers, even when clouds hid the sun?
And did her family try to force her to marry?
And did they treat her as a slave? Did it cost
her to keep herself like that all for love?

As she looked closer at the Virgin Wari carved
in wood, a twinkle of merriment came into her
dark eyes and a slow smile crept over her face.
Now if Tekakwitha could have made the statue
of the Mother of the Universe, she thought, she
would not have copied the blackrobe's Mother.
She would have made a squaw, an Algonquin
squaw, with a smiling face and a feather in her
hair.

Aunt Teedah went three times to the chapel
that day. As for Tekakwitha, she spent all the
time that she could spare warming her heart by
the Bethlehem manger, and each time she came
back lost in wonder, while snowflakes dropped in
tiny stars and wheels into her smooth black hair.
How she envied the Christians! Often that day

and in the days that followed, as she bent over her work, she fancied that the waters of baptism fell upon her head, gently, as the falling snow, bringing the grace for which she longed so much.

Years passed by, and with every one that passed, Tekakwitha felt the gulf grow wider and wider between her and Uncle Onsengongo. The slow poison of hate had deepened the lines in his face, for the departure of Christian Indians for the mission in Canada filled him with silent fury. Already 200 Mohawks had left their villages. Where would the old strength of the Iroquois be if this gospel of peace turned more of his good warriors into women? Even the Big Mohawk, Chief Kryn, had been converted and was traveling around preaching like any black-robe.

Father Boniface had died and his place had been taken by one of the saintliest priests of New France, Father Jacques de Lamberville, whom the Indians called Onesent. More and more the Iroquois were open to the Christian faith as the joy of the new converts spread like a good infection.

Father de Lamberville was a tired man, but he took no rest. Even when the springtime came and the Indians spent entire days out in the fields planting their new crops, he passed his time teaching those who were too old or too young to work. We're both sowing precious

seed, my Iroquois flock and I, he thought one
sunny morning in April as he went visiting from
lodge to lodge. He glanced up at a one-fire lodge
under a pine tree with a big red tortoise carved
on its gable front. Not once during the year he
had been at Kanawaki had he dared to enter
this one, but now he hesitated. It's no use going
in anyway, he told himself, as he passed by; all
the people are of working age.

"Father de Lamberville," a voice seemed to
say to him, "go back and visit that lodge."

He retraced his steps. As he reached the open
door, he fancied that the shadow of the terrible
old chief barred his way, but, Indian fashion,
he walked in without knocking.

Tekakwitha, now a slim young girl of eighteen, was seated on a mat making a belt, while
an old woman and two young girls kept her
company. At the sight of the priest a look of
joyful surprise lighted up her small, delicate face.
Slowly, and with difficulty, she rose, for an in-
jured foot had kept her from working in the
fields.

Oh, how often she had yearned to speak to
Onesent, to tell him all the thoughts and feelings
and longings of her heart! Yet, now that he was
here, for a moment there seemed to be no words
in her at all, not even a greeting—only the word-
less welcome of her soul that felt the goodness

and radiance of the spiritual world within him and reached out for it.

Humility and thankfulness were in her eyes, her slightly bowed head, her hands clasped before her as one who prays. For had not the Master of Life Himself sent Onesent? And what had she done to deserve so great a favor?

Neither the old woman nor the two girls tried to speak. They just stood silently watching the blackrobe and Tekakwitha because the lodge seemed suddenly only big enough for these two.

"Onesent," said Tekakwitha at last. "I have heard the Words of Life that you speak. My heart has been stirred. I want to be a Christian. I want to be baptized."

She did not wait for his reply. Truth itself was in his face, and under the serene and pure gaze of his understanding eyes, even her shyness gave way before the intense longing of her heart. Like a river that bursts its banks in spring from too much fullness, words now flowed from her lips. She told him of her struggles for purity, of her Christian mother, of the first visit of the blackrobes in Kanawaki and her secret desire to be a Christian, of her uncle's hatred of Christianity and of his fear that if she became one she, too, might leave for the mission in Canada.

Father de Lamberville listened in astonishment. Such meekness, and yet such courage and determination! He had expected to find only pagans in this lodge, and here was a young girl in whom he could see the grace of God already shining. But one must not act hastily. The suffering that was sure to come might break this frail body, for all her courage.

"My child," said the missionary gently, "think of the persecution . . ."

"I know what persecution is already, Onesent, and I am ready to face it. Have no fear for me. I have made up my mind, and nothing will persuade me to turn back. I must become a Christian even if I have to go somewhere else to receive this great grace."

She stopped speaking. It was all said now. It was like that time when she had refused to marry. Nothing could change this either. Nothing else in the whole world mattered but to step out of the darkness of paganism into the light of the Christian faith, cost what it might.

Father de Lamberville was quiet a moment, seeking guidance. "You will begin by praying, my child," he said at last. "God knows your desire and will grant it when it is His will. You may pray even as you work. Would your uncle mind if you went to the chapel now and then?"

"No, Onesent."

"Then go when you can be spared from your tasks." Quietly he blessed her and then left.

For a whole year Tekakwitha waited and

prayed. There were only two places in the village to which she went now—her lodge and the chapel.

At last the day of days arrived. Her uncle, who made no objection to her frequent visits to the chapel to pray with the Christians, sullenly, and to the surprise of everyone, gave his consent to her baptism. Safer to allow her, he thought. There's a core of stubbornness in this strange Algonquin girl, gentle though she is, and she might take a notion to leave me.

Easter Sunday was the day picked by Father de Lamberville for Tekakwitha's baptism because he felt the occasion was a very special one. While he had been teaching her, he had discovered a rare soul already blessed with heaven's most precious gifts.

"I am going to baptize you Catherine, Tekakwitha," he told her, "for then you will bear the name of a very great saint who loved purity as you do."

Tekekwitha glowed with humble happiness.

How festive the chapel was that Easter morning! All the Christians had taken pleasure in helping to make it beautiful for the baptism of the orphan girl. The men brought their richest furs of beaver, bear, silver fox and raccoon to decorate the walls. And the women gave necklaces, bracelets, and ornaments of all kinds and colors to make festoons.

How the people crowded in for the ceremony! Even some of the pagans came, for it was no small event to see the Tortoise Chief's adopted daughter baptized. In the hushed stillness that followed the hymns, all eyes watched with wonder and curiosity as Tekakwitha advanced into the holy place, her face alight with joy and peace, while Father de Lamberville waited for her with no less joyous an expression. "For it was the happiest day of my ministry," he said later.

Slowly Catherine Tekakwitha walked back to the lodge that morning, holding her happiness carefully in her heart as a child who carries a too-full cup. Even the birds sang more rapturously. Even the colors of the flowers burned more brightly, for it was the moon of the new leaf and all nature was in a state of grace.

9. Flight Through the Forest

"ALGONQUIN!" "CHRISTIAN!" MOCKING VOICES called from the woods as Tekakwitha made her way home from the spring with a jug of water on her shoulder.

A stone hurtled through the air, hitting her on the back of the head. She felt a blinding flash of pain and, for a moment, thought she must sink to the ground. With difficulty she steadied herself and took a tighter grip on her jug, pressing it close to her cheek as though for some protection.

If only she could see better! But the sun was full in her face and she had to hold her shawl across her eyes with her free arm.

She heard a swishing of leaves and a snapping of twigs as her tormentors came out of the woods. They were closing in behind her now. She could hear men's voices, and women's voices, and even the voices of children.

And children were always my friends! thought Tekakwitha.

She tried to quicken her pace, but it was no use. There was no strength in her today. Suddenly a child snatched her shawl and flung it to the ground with a shout of glee. Then a rough hand pushed her, jolting the jug from her shoulder. Water splashed down the front of her dress and into her moccasins as it fell.

"Are you baptized enough now, Algonquin?" jeered a harsh male voice. Shouts of laughter greeted this remark, and a volley of stones struck her in the back and legs.

Blinded by the sun and utterly defenseless, Tekakwitha stood alone, not knowing which way to turn. A shower of mud hit her full in the face and a stone cut her upper lip. She could feel warm blood trickling into her mouth and running down her chin. Dizzy and faint with pain, she fell to the ground.

As the group took to the woods again, the girl slowly struggled to her feet and reached for her empty jug and her shawl.

"It's nothing to what You suffered on Your way to Calvary," she said lovingly.

Painfully she dragged her feet all the way back to the spring. Here she would rest for a while before trying to go on. She sat down on the grass and leaned against the trunk of a tree. It was not the first time that she had been stoned, but always it left the body and all the nerves surprised and shocked.

A song sparrow cocked a beady eye at her and then fluted consolingly. A deer peeped at her through a screen of leaves, its great liquid eyes full of sympathy. One didn't run away from anyone as gentle as that; it bent its graceful head down and took a leisurely drink from the pool, looked at her once again, and then ambled away. One could always count on the kindness of the wild things, she thought, pressing her cheek against the rough bark of the tree.

Gradually the silence and the rest soothed her, and her heart beat less wildly. She got up, took her jug to the brink of the pool, and knelt down, meaning to fill it. But as her eyes looked into the clear, pure water, such a tide of love and joy flooded her heart that she no longer felt any pain in her body. For several moments she remained there, still as a statue, lost in prayer, lost to all earthly things of now and here. Then, after what seemed like an eternity of bliss, she became aware again of the pain, the pool, the forest, her empty jug in her hands.

"What a muddy face!" she exclaimed as she bent over to fill the jug. She set it down full and, cupping her two hands in the water, doused her face and neck.

I'll take the trail down near the river this time, she said to herself. They might be waiting again.

She set her jug on her shoulder and began to walk slowly back to the village, feeling the scald of her wounds and the ache of her bones with every step. My people tell their prisoners they are caressing them when they beat them, she thought. They say this to mock them, but it is true when one suffers for love. A faint smile hovered on her lips. I am covered with caresses today, she told herself.

At the top of a little hill near the river she paused. Two canoes were just pushing off from the shore. As they paddled into mid-stream the Indians began to sing a hymn.

It's the party of Christians going off to the mission in Canada, she thought. Wistfully she gazed after them until a grave voice called, "Catherine," and she turned around to see Father de Lamberville.

"Onesent!"

At the sight of her, Father de Lamberville winced. How shockingly tired she looked, and they had been stoning her again!

"You are hurt, my child," he said kindly.

"It is nothing, Onesent. I have been . . ."

"Then why are you crying?"

Quickly she brushed away her tears with the back of her hand.

"I was just thinking how beautiful it must be at the mission in Canada where everyone loves Iesos and all are brothers and sisters in Him."

"You look half starved, Catherine. Have you eaten today?"

"Not yet. Onesent knows we do not eat until the sun is over there."

"Yesterday?"

"No. Yesterday was the Lord's Day. I do not eat on the Lord's Day."

"But, Catherine, you must not fast a whole day. No one may fast like that without permission."

"I do not do this wilfully, Onesent. They will not give me food on the Lord's Day because on that day I cannot go to work in the fields. They say I have become lazy since I was baptized." A look of pain came into the girl's eyes.

Father de Lamberville looked anxiously toward the village. "I shall go with you part of the way," he said gently.

For a few moments he walked silently by her

side. O, God! how hard it was to see so frail a child abused like this! How he wished he could make an exception for her and give her the Blessed Sacrament now, instead of making her wait for years like the other Indians. She was far more ready to receive this great grace than so many Christians at home in France.

"Catherine," he said at last, "would you like to go to the mission in Canada?"

She glanced quickly over her shoulder, fearful lest someone should have heard. "Oh, Onesent, I cannot go. Never would my uncle consent to my leaving!"

"Your cross is heavy, my child, but are you happy?"

"Oh, so happy sometimes, Onesent. It is as though . . ." Tears of gratitude brimmed her eyes. "There is only one thing that I am afraid of."

"What is that?"

"That I may not have the courage to let them kill me rather than work on the Lord's Day."

"Have they threatened to kill you?"

"Yes, Onesent."

"I think they will not do this, Catherine. But if it happens you will be given courage. Our Lord seldom gives us things in advance. Now you will be safe the rest of the way. *Onan*, Catherine, and God bless you."

"*Onan*, Onesent."

It was quiet when she entered the lodge, for everyone was out. How good the food smelled! The others had eaten, but they had left some for her on the fire. Without stopping to fill her bowl, she took a big ladle of *sagamite* and wolfed it down. Then another and another. But no sooner had she eaten than pain seized her. She went over to her mat and, when the sharpest of the pains had passed, took up a piece of embroidery.

I wonder what I can remember of the litany of the Blessed Virgin Wari, she said to herself. Quietly she began to recite it: "Mother so pure; Mother so chaste . . ." One by one the beautiful titles followed each other in a quiet rhythm. When she came to the words, "mystical rose," she paused. It must be all white like the blossom I saw in the pool with the three drops of water, she thought, but with no roots.

At the sound of a heavy tread, she looked up. A rough, fierce-looking man, naked to the waist and armed with a tomahawk, entered her lodge.

"Christian," he shouted as he strode toward her, "give up your faith or I'll kill you!"

Every little pulse in her body became a danger signal, but she did not move or utter a cry. She caught a glimpse of the tomahawk as he swung it up over his head.

Quietly she bowed her head, while deep within

the peaceful center of her being she heard the words, "Help of Christians . . ."

But what had this wild man seen that so suddenly filled him with terror? He sprang back from her, dropping the tomahawk. Turning around, he rushed headlong from the lodge as though Otkon, the devil, were after him.

Now Tekakwitha could no longer even go to church by the usual path. Always there would be a trap laid for her—rough people waiting to throw stones at her, drunken men, or men pretending to be drunk, who would fall on her as though to strike her.

As things went from bad to worse, her wistful dreams of the new Eden at the mission in Canada sharpened into a great longing. Every time a canoe of Christians went off, she would watch, the tears rolling down her cheeks, her heart swollen with grief. Anastasia, her mother's friend, was there now, and her cousin, too, and oh! what a heaven it must be to be able to worship the Master of Life and His Son Iesos in perfect freedom! Aunt Teedah did not mind if she left—she had said so—but Uncle Onsengongo! I think he would kill me first, Tekakwitha told herself.

At last the crisis came. It was after the special ceremony in honor of the Blessed Virgin Wari that the persecutions were redoubled, for the jugglers loathed the Mother of the Universe for reducing their riches and ruining their trade.

Daily they lay in wait for Tekakwitha, shaking their rattles at her and threatening her whenever she passed by.

One day, as she was collecting roots for dyeing, she heard a crack of twigs behind her and the Crooked-mouth Doctor leaped out at her and pitched all his weight against her body. As the horrible wooden mask struck her cheek, she could smell his odious breath reeking of brandy. She struggled wildly, but he threw her to the ground. Then, hearing a party of people, he dashed out of sight into the thicket.

Tekakwitha picked herself up, trembling with fright. Leaving her basket where it was, she ran for the village. Where was Onesent? At the church? At the lodge where he stayed? In her blind haste she nearly knocked him over outside of the chapel.

"Onesent!" she cried, but no words followed, just wild sobs that shook her frail little body.

"It's the jugglers, Onesent!" she said at last. "They terrify me. Oh, Onesent, I'm afraid. I'm afraid for . . ."

"My child, don't you think you should go to the mission?"

"Yes, Onesent, yes!"

Then suddenly she became very calm, and the look of quiet determination that Father de Lamberville had seen before came into her face. "I must go, Onesent. I shall go, yes, even if they kill me for it!"

"I think God has provided a way, Catherine," said Father de Lamberville, "but we must act with the greatest caution. You will say nothing to anyone?"

"Nothing, Onesent."

"A converted chief is coming from the mission tomorrow. You have heard of Hot Ashes, the captain of the Oneidas?"

"The one who tortured the good blackrobe Brébeuf and who ate his heart?"

"Yes, Catherine. He is coming here to preach. I shall ask him to help you to escape. Go now; there are people coming this way. *Onan.*"

When Hot Ashes arrived, Father de Lamberville took him first to the chapel where they prayed together. Then he told him about Catherine.

"That's strange," said Hot Ashes. "One of the Christian Indians with me is Kahriio, her cousin's husband. How well the Lord of Life plans things! I, myself, must go on to preach to the Oneidas tomorrow; she can take my place in the canoe with the Huron and her relative."

Father de Lamberville smiled with relief. "Blessed be God!" he said, "and the old man, her uncle, has gone down to Albany to trade with the English."

That night the big council house was packed

with Christians and pagans. All the old men were there, their stubborn, weather-beaten faces a study in curiosity and scorn. Solemnly they drew on their calumets, eying the one-time warrior and drinker of firewater with silent unbelief.

"Once I lived like a beast," Hot Ashes was saying, "but now that I have come to know the Great Spirit, the true Master of heaven and earth, I live like a man." After his sermon he went on to describe the beautiful life at the mission, where they lived like brothers and sisters of one family, sharing all they had with one another and, best of all, sharing the Bread of Life.

One by one the elders got up and left the lodge. Others stayed to mock or ask questions. But the most eager of all Hot Ashes' listeners was Tekakwitha.

All that night she lay awake, waiting for the dawn. When the very first glimmer of light showed through the smoke hole she got up, fetched a basket with her few little possessions from the shed, and hurried down through the door of the stockade, not daring to glance back over her shoulder.

The meeting place was at the spring on the outskirts of the village. How endless the way seemed this morning! Every bush and tree seemed to hide an enemy, and the slightest rustle of leaves or the fall of a seed pod made her heart pound.

Father de Lamberville was waiting for her with a happy smile but, as he talked to her in undertones, his eyes kept anxiously scanning the countryside.

He took a letter from his pocket. "My child, you will give this to the blackrobe when you arrive. Keep it safely."

She placed the letter in her basket. Little did she guess its contents: "You will soon discover the treasure I am sending you. Guard it well."

There was no time for delay. With a fervent prayer for her safety, he gave her his last blessing. "May the Mother of our blessed Lord accompany and protect you, Catherine," he said, as he walked with her to where Kahriio and the Huron were waiting at the riverside.

My own mother, too, thought Tekakwitha. She traveled this same journey when she came as a slave to Ossernenon. How frightened she, too, must have been!

"*Onan*, Onesent," she whispered, as she knelt in the canoe and picked up a paddle. Through tears she took a last look at the saintly figure on the shore. Then the canoe shot out into the river, so swiftly that it sounded like corn sheaths being stripped from the cob.

As they got out of sight of the village, the rim of the rising sun, round and ruddy as the rind of a pumpkin, flared at the edge of the forest.

They'll know I'm gone now, thought Tekakwitha. I wonder when Uncle Onsengongo will get back.

Down at Fort Albany the Tortoise Chief sat at a counter beside his pelts and handmade goods, slowly drinking brandy.

"Those blackrobes and French," the rosy-cheeked English trader was saying, "you'll have to get rid of them if you ever want to become a strong nation again." He filled up the chief's mug. After a suitable amount of liquor and anti-French talk, one could drive a good bargain, he thought, as he eyed a pair of exquisitely embroidered moccasins. Now what woman's clever hands had made those?

As the Tortoise Chief downed the second mug, his bleary eyes blinked at the shiny pails, axes, blankets, bright new knives, and guns ranged around the store. He shoved his empty mug aside and stumped over to the pails, picking one up to examine it. Pails and blankets it would be this time.

At that moment the door of the store was flung open and a Mohawk came bolting in, hot and breathless.

"She's gone," he said to the chief in a low voice. "Your niece . . . she ran away. Her cousin's husband and another Christian who came with Hot Ashes took her off in their canoe."

"Gone!" snarled the Tortoise Chief, his eyes blazing with rage.

"You may still have time to catch up to them if you beat upstream fast enough. They've taken the river route, knowing you'd be here for a few days."

The pail clattered from the old chief's hand. "I want a gun," he roared at the trader, "and plenty of shot."

"Twenty beaver skins for one gun," said the trader coolly.

With wild hands the chief fumbled among his furs. "Ten beaver skins and all the other stuff," he said, "for one good gun and the bullets."

"It's a bargain," said the trader, handing over a brand-new musket and some shot.

Hastily the Tortoise Chief loaded it and clicked back the lock. A few minutes later he was in his canoe paddling desperately up the river. There was a sound like a distant rapid in his ears, and the blood surged in his veins like a river at flood time.

I'd recognize Kahriio a mile off, he told himself. Squaw Christian! If I get my hands on him, I'll strangle him!

Blind with fury, he glanced up at an approaching canoe. In it was Kahriio, on his way to the nearest Dutch village to get bread for Tekakwitha and the Huron, hiding in the bush. It came nearer; it passed within a few paddle lengths of him . . .

"And he didn't seem to know me!" Kahriio told the others later when he rejoined them. "I just acted as innocent as an owl. But we have no time to lose. He's fuming and he has a gun. When he doesn't cross us higher up, he'll come back after us. Look, Tekakwitha, when we reach the portage, you'll walk behind the Huron and I'll come up last. If I see him coming, the signal will be a gunshot. Duck down into some thick bushes and freeze. I'll dive into the woods as though after some game I've shot, and you," he pointed to the Huron, "he doesn't know you. Just look innocent and cool."

Arrived at the portage, they cached the canoe in some rushes and silently took the trail through the forest, Tekakwitha praying at every step of the way. Somehow running away from Uncle Onsengongo made him seem all the more big and fearsome, so that it was as though a huge giant, with a voice like thunder, were chasing after her.

Suddenly the sharp report of a gun ripped its way through the silence. Tekakwitha stumbled and almost fell. Then, running for the nearest clump of underbrush, she threw herself into it. She could hear the crashing of bushes as Kahriio dashed into the woods. At the sound of the shot, the Huron had squatted by the side of the trail. Peering through the leaves, she could see him now, calmly lighting his calumet. There was a moment of terrifying suspense. Then the huge figure of the Tortoise Chief loomed ahead on the forest path.

Nearer and nearer he came on swift, silent moccasins, so near now that she could see his bloodshot eyes.

At the sight of the Huron, he advanced toward him.

"*Sago*," said the old man dryly. "Did you see a young squaw and two men ahead of you?"

The Huron stretched his legs and gazed dreamily after a thin scarf of blue smoke, then slowly shook his head.

There was something about this young man comfortably smoking that made the old chief feel a sharp longing for rest. What's the use, he thought. They're all young, too, young and nimble and no doubt miles away by now. Mournfully he eyed the trail ahead, then turned around and began to trudge doggedly back the way he had come.

At the river, he paused to splash water on his damp, hot head. It was clear now, clear and empty of everything but discouragement.

Perhaps it's just a mistake, he told himself, as he paddled slowly back to Kanawaki.

Out in the yard, Aunt Teedah was dehairing a hide. At the sight of him she glanced up but said nothing.

It's true, he thought. She's sorry, but she's not angry. How old she looks today, my squaw!

Without a word he stumped into the lodge, sat down, and lit his calumet. All his anger had been used up in the chase, and now a sense of loss that was new and very strange to Uncle Onsengongo crept stealthily into his heart. He pulled savagely on his pipe. "I must be getting old myself," he muttered.

10. The Praying Castle

EVERYTHING WAS RACING THAT AUTUMN day. The clouds were racing. And the wind was racing through the trees, setting the tiny aspen leaves aquiver. And the canoe carrying Tekakwitha and Kahriio and the Huron fairly danced over the choppy waters of the lake en route to the Promised Land.

Once beyond the danger of discovery, Tekakwitha had finished the trip along the forest trail as though wings were attached to her feet. Her mat at night was a bed of moss or leaves, and her food, just what they could pick up. Her back ached and her eyes ached and there was the old pain in the pit of her stomach, but there was never a word of complaint—only continual praise to the Lord of Life, for her heart was a singing bird escaped from a snare, and Love was the theme.

At the end of the trail they had found the canoe hidden by Hot Ashes and his two companions on the trip up, and it was in this that they were now traveling over the lake named by Father Jogues the Blessed Sacrament, and by the English, Lake George.

Even in the midst of her joy, Tekakwitha seemed to be seeing everything with Kahenta's eyes. Had her mother seen that great fir tree there on the point, standing like a giant chief, or that little shining bay curved like a crescent moon? And oh, poor Mother, she thought. She was leaving a Christian village behind and going to live among strangers and pagans. How her heart must have ached on this long journey, not knowing what would become of her!

By the time they reached Lake Champlain, Indian summer had set in, with its windless, golden weather. How the woods cried with color! Long banners of scarlet and yellow, emerald and amethyst reached down into the still lake, and

Tekakwitha's heart leaped with delight to see, here and there, the reflection of a white birch bole cleaving the water like forked lightning. Raweniio made us Indians for prayer, she thought. We are always kneeling—in our fields, by our streams, in our canoes. . . . And who could look at all this beauty without kneeling in adoration before the Creator of all things? For it seemed to her that the whole world was one great tabernacle filled with the Living Presence.

From Lake Champlain they paddled down the Richelieu River for a few miles and then left the chain of waterways for another long trek through the forest. At last they came to the banks of the mightiest river Tekakwitha had ever seen.

"That's the St. Lawrence," said Kahriio. He hauled a canoe from a clump of bushes and dragged it to the water. "It's homeward bound now, Catherine, because our home is yours. My wife and Anastasia will be overjoyed to see you. For a long time they've been praying you would come."

"It is good of you to have me," said Tekakwitha, with a heart too full for more words.

The long journey of 200 miles was nearly ended. As they paddled up the great waterway of Canada, the men sang their hymns. But Tekakwitha was silent, tasting her new freedom with rare happiness and feeling with it the urgent call to a higher and a holier life.

"There it is!" cried Kahriio. "Look, Catherine!" Then, seeing the girl's still face and the veiled look in her eyes, he remembered her short sight. "It's the Praying Castle. You'll be able to see it in just a few minutes," he said.

The mission! They had arrived at last! Tears swam in the girl's eyes and her heart seemed ready to burst for joy. As they drew nearer, the river widened out into a lake, and she could hear a distant, thunderous roar of water rolling over in rapids and cascades of foam.

Soon she could see the mission for herself high up on a hill—the wooden fort circling the church and the missionaries' house, and the sprawling longhouses scattered pell-mell around it. Just a humble Indian village, but to Tekakwitha it was like the "new Jerusalem come down from God out of heaven."

A group of people who had been watching the approaching canoe came hurrying down to meet the travelers. Among them was her cousin, Katentas, and behind her, Anastasia, eager for tidbits of news from Mohawk country and especially of her dear Tekakwitha.

The canoe turned and pointed shoreward. There were shouts of greeting and then a wild little cry of sheer surprise and joy. "Why, it's Tekakwitha! It's my little girl!" And the next moment Tekakwitha was hugged in Anastasia's motherly arms and fairly smothered with kisses.

"Oh, but you're more like your mother than ever!" she exclaimed, as she held her off to get a better look at her. "But you're not so strong as she was. Such thin little arms and legs! You'll need to wrap up warmly in the cold Canadian winters."

Kahriio laughed. "Who says she's not strong, Anastasia! She can run like a deer when a big bear is after her. We nearly lost her once."

"And I've never seen a girl paddle faster than she did on the Mohawk the morning we left," said the Huron.

Katentas put her arm around Tekakwitha's waist. "We've always kept a place for you in our lodge, Little Cousin," she said warmly.

They were all chattering so much as they climbed the hill that no one but Tekakwitha noticed the blackrobe coming toward them. Her face lighted up with a happy smile of recognition, for it was Father Frémin.

"Well, well!" he said, beaming with pleasure. "Surely this is the little Iroquois princess who gave me my first meal in Kanawaki and who used to sometimes listen in on my sermons."

"*Sago*, Raguenni," said Tekakwitha shyly, using the word Father, instead of Blackrobe, for the first time. It was so like a real homecoming! She reached into her basket for the letter.

Quietly Father Frémin read it. I guessed as much long ago, he mused, as he looked down into the small, sensitive face and the eyes that seemed to hold a heavenly secret. The same sweetness and eagerness in the young woman as in the child, he thought, and something else—something rare, something very rare!

"Well, you have her here at last, Anastasia," he said, seeing the maternal glow in the older woman's face. "You always did want a daughter, didn't you?"

"A daughter's a comfort to a widowed woman, Father," she said.

"And I can recommend her as a good cook," said Father Frémin. "What is your baptized name, Tekakwitha?"

"Catherine."

"Good."

How bright the gold shines from the fires of suffering, he thought, as he walked away. There's a firmness in her now, as well as gentleness.

"I expect we shall all call you Kateri," said Anastasia, as they went on into the lodge.

The girl laughed. "So many names I have had!" she exclaimed. "But the sweetest of all was the one they called me at Kanawaki since my baptism."

"What was that?" asked Katentas.

"Christian," said Tekakwitha. "Iesos Cristos—it's the nearest to His name."

How soundly Kateri slept that night! Early in the morning she was awakened by a new and strange noise. Where am I? she wondered, battling for a second against a tide of confused impressions. Then, as she remembered, she took a deep and joyous breath.

Dingdong! Dingdong!

"That's the church bell, Kateri," explained Anastasia, who was already moving about. "It's ringing for the first Mass. We're all going to thank Raweniio for bringing you safely to us."

A few minutes later they were walking through the ghostly light of early dawn. Once Kateri looked nervously back over her shoulder. Then she laughed. "Oh, Anastasia, I'm not used to walking to church peacefully like this," she said.

Anastasia glanced affectionately at her companion. "You know, Kateri," she said, "when you got out of that canoe yesterday, I could just see your poor mother when she arrived at Ossernenon with all the warriors."

"How happy she must be in heaven today!" said the girl. "I felt the protection of her prayers all the way."

The two were silent for a few moments. Then Kateri touched her friend's arm. "Anastasia," she said, "I should like to call you Mother. You were always the nearest to her. And you will teach me to become a good Christian like her."

Anastasia's answer was a warm smile and a nod, for they were at the church door now. Quietly they took their places among the ranks of kneeling Christians, going to the epistle side which was reserved for the women. Although it was not yet five o'clock, many Indians were already at the church, and some had been there since four o'clock. In utter silence Father Frémin entered with the chalice. With what eagerness and fervor the Indians followed the Holy Sacrifice!

Kateri watched all this with wonder and awe. She was touched to tears to see Iroquois, Hurons, Algonquins and three or four other tribes who would, at one time, have taken each other's scalps, meekly waiting side by side at the communion rail. It was a scene that often moved Father Frémin, too. It's like the prophet Isaiah's vision of the millenium, he thought—the wolf and the lamb, the leopard, the kid and the bear, all together. Just a little difference in the totems! Today, as he turned toward his flock for the *Ite Missa Est*, another text from Isaiah lay in the back of his mind: "They shall not hurt nor destroy in all my holy mountain; for the earth shall be full of the knowledge of the Lord, as the waters cover the sea."

Father Cholenec said the second Mass at six. None of those who had attended the first left, but others poured into the chapel until everyone in the whole village was there. Daily Mass was always attended like this at the Sault mission. Besides, there were the frequent visits to the Blessed

Sacrament coming from and going to the fields, and then prayers all together in the evening.

"The whole village could be taken for a monastery," wrote the astonished bishop after a visit to the mission. And it was not just outward piety but the patient practice of virtue. Willingly and joyously the Christians shared their goods with the poor and the sick. Often, when newcomers arrived, the older Christians gave up their own fruitful lands to them and themselves took on the hard work of breaking new soil. Instead of complaining, the sick thanked God for testing them. Some, like Hot Ashes, went back to the pagan villages as apostles, risking mockery and even torture and death to win others to the faith.

Daily Kateri's heart warmed to this beautiful spiritual climate. And her soul, already sown with precious seeds of truth, grew and blossomed as a watered garden in springtime. The very air she breathed seemed purer to her, and the grandeur of the landscape lifted her thoughts to God. For all nature seemed to share in the cleansing wind of redemption that had swept through the souls of the Indian people. And all this beauty without and within was a free gift from the Heart of Love Who had created and redeemed her. Love and joy were the total response of her being. They were in her winning laughter, in her song, and in her long silences. She wove them into the beautiful patterns and colors of her embroidery and kneaded them into her bread. Even the humblest little tasks were rainbow-tinted with them.

And since the Great Lover had taken such pains to leave His symbols and messages for her in nature, she answered in the same language. In the bark of the trees along the path to the spring she carved crosses, and at the spring itself, that ever-enchanting place, she made a little shrine so that each trip with her jug could be a pilgrimage of love.

Seldom was she out of Anastasia's presence, so hungry was she to learn more of the truths of the faith and the lives of the saints. One of the commonest sights at the Sault was to see her and her old companion and teacher side by side in the fields and the forests, or walking to and from the church, rosaries in hand, quietly talking together.

For Anastasia, these precious hours spent with her pupil were one sweet surprise of discovery, almost unbelievable at times. During those first days and weeks at the Sault she could scarcely keep up with her pupil. "Why, she learns more in one week than the others do in several years," she told Father Cholenec.

"That's because she has such a good teacher," said the blackrobe.

Anastasia looked pleased but shook her head. "The teacher is learning many things from her pupil," she said humbly. "I believe she lives constantly in the presence of God."

"What would you say, Anastasia, if we were to give Catherine her first Communion on Christmas Day?" asked Father Cholenec.

"Oh, Father, I cannot imagine her joy. Have you really decided this?"

Father Cholenec smiled and nodded. "You may tell her yourself if you like," he said.

The first snow was falling when Anastasia found Kateri. She was down by the big cross on the banks of the river where she loved so much to pray and meditate. She did not notice the older woman's approach. At the touch of a hand on her shoulder, the younger one turned and looked into the kindly eyes of her friend and teacher. Anastasia always marveled a little and felt a stranger to that look in the girl's face when she had been alone praying.

"I have good news for you, Kateri," she said softly. "The blackrobes have decided to give you the Blessed Sacrament on Christmas Day."

A smile lit up the girl's whole face, but she did not speak. She just laid her hand on Anastasia's arm while the moment's joy stretched out into eternity. Together they walked back to the lodge. It was snowing more now. Flake upon faltering flake fell around them like a soft communion veil. It had been like this once long ago, far away in Kanawaki—the snow . . . Father Boniface . . . the Virgin Wari, with the child Iesos . . . and the longing in her heart for grace. And now there was another longing, and with it a promise. This Christmas her own heart would be the manger, a tabernacle for the living Iesos as truly as the Virgin Wari's flesh and blood.

Christmas Day did dawn at last for Kateri with the sweet sound of church bells calling across the white, frozen world, the gentle radiance of candle-light in the chapel, and the voices of the Indians singing the carols that seemed to have been born in paradise:

> "Within a lodge of broken bark
> The tender Babe was found;
> A ragged robe of rabbit skin
> Enwrapped His beauty round . . .
> While chiefs from far before Him knelt
> With gifts of fox and beaver pelt . . ."

Once again, as for her baptism, the people had vied with each other to make the church beautiful with furs and ornaments, for this was a very special Christmas for everyone at the Sault. There was not only the private joy of each one; none could help but catch a little of the rapture and glow from Kateri's loving and expectant heart.

The cup of her happiness had been full to the brim at her baptism. It was overflowing now. From that time forward she appeared different from everyone else because she remained so full of God and of love for Him.

11. Crown of Thorns

How BRIGHT THE WINTER WOODS SHONE that morning with the sun lighting up the tips of the snowy trees like candles and glistening on the icy ponds. And what fun it was for the families of the tortoise, the wolf, and the bear to be out for the chase, tingling with eagerness for the tracking of their four-footed cousins—the beaver, the moose, the martin, and the deer. For the hunting season had come round again, and the

Indians of the Sault were out in the forest making their way group by group to their favorite camping grounds.

For nights before they had left, young Christian braves had been dreaming of war and scalping and had wakened to find it was happily untrue. But the thirst for adventure, for struggle, for something against which they could pit their muscles and sinews was as alive in them as ever, and the chase was a form of warfare that they still adored.

Hooting and shouting with laughter until the forest rang with merriment, they padded swiftly along on silent snowshoes. Sometimes a young brave would put a birch-bark horn to his lips, imitating the cry of an animal—the deep baritone call of a bull moose or the crooning welcome of its mate. Many a beast in search of romance had been lured to death this way.

The young squaws, too, were in bubbling high spirits. Now and then one would roll the other in the thick snow while the rest laughed to see her scramble up all white and tousled and looking like a young bear after a tussle.

Who would want to be back at the Sault, sitting by the fire like the ancient ones, when they could be out like this in the sunlight and among the soft blue shadows with the clean, cold perfume of the snow in their nostrils and the prospect of three months of blissful idleness, brightened by pleasant gossip and feasting? Who but one young girl of twenty-one, whose dark eyes were dim, but who had been so blinded to all earthly pleasures by the Light Divine that she had left her heart behind her near the tabernacle where it would evermore belong?

But she would not make a misery of her sacrifice. Wholeheartedly she joined in the fun, glad that it was wholesome and clean. It was all so different from the trips to the forest with the pagans, when drunkenness and debauchery had disgusted her and made her feel lonely and a stranger even among her own people.

The Christian Indians did not leave their faith and piety behind at the mission. Tucked away safely among the packs, in two bark containers, were the portable means of grace prepared by the blackrobes for each group. One of these contained birch-bark scrolls with daily prayers, and the other, the Church calendar showing the various feast days and days on which the Indians must tighten their beaded belts for the love of their Lord.

With the setting up of the rough bark lodges, the hunt began in earnest. Young blood pounded in the veins while, with gun or bow and arrow, the Indians chased the animals down twisted lanes of wind and snow, or stalked silently up to surprise them in their lairs and burrows. "You fine bear!" or "You great hulking moose!" they would sometimes address them, giving them a little sermon on the splendor of courage as they watched them die. For the Indian had a great respect for the wild creatures, and not just on account of the meat and the hides.

With the young squaws Kateri scooted through the forest, following the tracks of the hunters in the snow or the signs they left to show where the game could be found, and bringing it back to the lodge. But apart from that, and the fetching of wood and water, life in the woods was a holiday for the squaws, compared with the regular routine at the mission. No bells to awaken them early for the Mass, no Benediction, no work in the fields, but long, lazy, carefree hours in the cosy, warm lodges where they could amuse themselves with games and chatter to their hearts' content.

For Kateri a life of idleness held no charm at all. The closer she came to God, the more she filled her life with work, looking upon each little task as a divine opportunity and a chance to remain united with Him.

The embroidery of collars, the preparation of furs for clothing or commerce, the treatment of birch bark for making furniture and canoes, and prayer filled every waking moment of her day.

"Why do you work so hard, Kateri?" the others would sometimes ask. And she would just smile and say, "Because I really love work as much as you love play." And they were pleased enough at that, for she took on all the hard work of the lodge and that left them more time for fun.

Sweetly and simply she offered each passing minute to Eternal Love. "Let's sing a hymn," she would say to her young companions, trying by gentle ways to help them sanctify some of their leisure hours and lift their thoughts heavenward. Or, "Please tell me the story of a saint. You all know so much more than I do because I have just come." And then the room would be all quiet, except for the crackling of the fires, while one of the older squaws would tell the story.

One day it would be about Saint Aloysius Gonzaga who rolled on thorns that his soul might find the singing purity it craved. Or it might be about Saint Genevieve of the blackrobe's country. But most of all Kateri loved Saint Francis of Assisi, the humble brother who felt too unworthy to become a priest, but preached sermons to the birds and the squirrels and the rabbits.

Spellbound, she heard how this gentle lover of birds and beasts had received the marks of the crucified Christ in his hands and feet and side. And as she listened, she knew that the human heart was made for everlasting happiness and that it began here and now. As the story went on, her longing to be a saint was so great that it seemed it was she who ran through the streets of Assisi weeping because Love was not loved. And the half-blind eyes of the saint lifted to heaven as he added a last verse to his beautiful *Hymn to the Sun* were her own sick eyes, as the joy in him was her own heart's joy.

The short winter days' stories and feasting and work and fun came to a close. Night enfolded the camp in its black bearskin, beaded with stars. After the evening prayers together the hunters, weary with the chase, and the squaws, nodding with drowsiness, would roll themselves luxuriously in their snug furs and fall into a peaceful slumber. But Kateri stayed up alone, praying by the dying fire, a shabby shawl wrapped around her frail shoulders. First she would begin with the litany of the Blessed Virgin and then, lifted up on wings of love and joy to the high places, she would remain lost in adoration. Hour after hour would pass by until at last sleep and cold overcame her body.

But in spite of the long night's vigil, she was the first up in the camp. Quietly she would slip past her sleeping companions and out into the cold.

The first red glow of sunrise would be glistening among the frosty trees as she made her way to her secret oratory. It was at the end of a narrow trail by a little stream. Fir and pine cloistered it in, and on one of these she had placed a large wooden cross.

How silent it was here! Except for a few frozen birds or a wild rabbit, her only companions were the trees. Quiet and contemplative, they stood around her muffled up in their white robes.

Like homing pigeons, her thoughts would fly to a point in space beyond the forest, beyond the frozen St. Lawrence River, where a blackrobe was making his way through the cold dawn to the church. Kneeling down in the snow before the cross, she would unite her heart and mind with his, following in every detail each part of the Mass and asking her guardian angel to bring her the fruits of it.

Before her on a level bank the snow lay like a smooth white altar cloth. Slowly the sun rose higher, lifted up like a dazzling Host to the glory of God. And the cross, coated with snow and ice, grew luminous in its rays.

Toward the end of the hunting season, as Kateri's need for solitude grew, her visits to this shrine became more frequent.

"Where does our Kateri go?" teased the young squaws. "I'm sure she has a secret lover." And Kateri, who wished above all to hide her acts of piety, would make no answer but just smile and bend her head over her work.

"See, she is blushing!" they would cry. "It must be Hawk Eye!" "Or Eagle Feather!" "She is so much in love that she forgets to eat now."

They did not know that she remained away at the big meal of the day in order to fast and that when she came back for a bowl of soup or *sagamite* she would mix some ashes with it that it might lose its flavor. But who could ever guess such things when the sweetness of sacrifice left her face as radiant and full of tenderness as a girl in love for the first time?

Little did she know that a cruel cross was in store for her and that soon she would bear the wounds of the crucified Christ not in her hands and feet and side like the good St. Francis, but in the most sensitive part of her soul.

One evening Enneta's husband, Occuna, did not return with the other hunters. A gamy moose had led him so far away in the chase that he did not get back to the lodge until even Kateri was asleep. Utterly exhausted, he sank down on the nearest unoccupied mat. At the first peep of dawn, Enneta awoke, restless and still anxious. Where was Occuna? Had he come back yet? She looked at the mat next to hers. It was empty. What had become of him? Should she rouse the others? She sat up and looked around her at the sleepers. Over by the door, and right next to Kateri's mat, was Occuna, fast asleep. Kateri had already risen and gone out as usual.

For the first time in twenty years of married life, a dark suspicion entered Enneta's heart, but she made no remark.

Late that afternoon Occuna appeared at the door of the lodge. "I need a squaw to put some stitches in a canoe," he called. "Will you help me, Kateri?" And Kateri, always ready to lend a willing hand, went off with him to the woods.

Now suspicions swarmed like hornets in Enneta's head. Kateri's constant absences, her indifference to food, and most of all that look of secret happiness in her face—were not all these clear signs of falling in love? And Occuna—he had tired of her now that she was older. He wanted the love of a young squaw.

Instead of asking for an explanation from her husband or Kateri, she said nothing but quietly nursed her grievance and decided to let the blackrobe speak to Kateri.

The return to the mission was like another homecoming after a long exile for Kateri. Soon I shall have a second Communion, she thought joyously, as she made her way to the missionary's house at Father Frémin's summons. She looked up brightly as he entered. But what was this shadow on the blackrobe's face? He paused a moment after greeting her. Never had he had so hard a task, for now in her presence, he felt more certain than ever of her innocence. Yet Enneta was an old and devout Christian woman and, unless he took notice of her complaint, he could never satisfy her nor silence the gossip that had already begun. Briefly he told Kateri the story as it had been given to him.

She listened quietly. In the still, serene expression of her face there was no flicker of emotion—nothing to show the agony of the wound opening under the thrust of the spear. When she had been very young she had cried bitterly at any accusation touching her purity. But now, like everything else about her, even her tears were a gift. They were for repentance for any wound she, or her tribe, might have caused to Love. They were for Love Itself and the five wounds of the cross.

Father Frémin ceased speaking. "Is it true, Catherine?" he asked.

Her eyes met his in a level look. "It is not true, my Father," she said with quiet dignity. And that was all. In the complete silence that followed, the blackrobe felt awkward and embarrassed.

Kateri's pain did not end there. In the whispered conversations at her approach, the droop of eyelids, the turning away of a head to hide a look of suspicion, she discovered that her supposed guilt was common knowledge at the mission. Enneta could not be persuaded of her innocence. Did Anastasia also suspect her? Did Katentas? They said nothing directly, but often in the midst of an ordinary conversation she had a feeling of being watched.

They accused You falsely too, she thought,
and that was enough for her warm and generous
heart. Taking her cup of suffering in both hands,
she offered it to the Beloved Lover, marveling
to find that the cross changed all to joy. For it
was the suffering that brought Love closer to her
and the loving that gave a meaning to all suffering and even made her wish for more.

Holy Week came. Her own wounds entirely
forgotten, she followed the Passion of Christ,
unable to restrain her tears whenever anyone
spoke of His sufferings.

And all this time the beauty and the sweetness
of her life had not gone unnoticed, either by
the Indians or the blackrobes. They had been
touched by her matchless courage under the cruel
test, her gentle graciousness, especially to those
who had hurt her the most, her magnificent self-
forgetfulness. Such heroism was not to go without
its reward.

"Catherine," called Father Frémin, as she was
leaving the church on Easter Sunday.

"Raguenni!" The joy of the Resurrection was
in that unshadowed smile.

"How would you like to belong to the Congregation of the Holy Family?"

Touched by this open tribute to her virtue, the
girl flushed with pleasure, and then her face became very serious. Only the most devout Christian women belonged to this group, and then

only after many years. "But, my Father," she protested, "I am not worthy of so great an honor."

That very day in the presence of Father Frémin, Father Cholenec, and Father Chauchetière, Kateri was made a member of the congregation. Instead of making her proud, it made her more humble. How could she do otherwise than bow her head to receive this crown of loving kindness from Iesos? He had planned it for her so that the others might believe in her purity, and He was telling her in this way that He wanted her to live a more perfect life.

Only Enneta harbored the shadow of a doubt about Kateri's innocence. But a day was coming when she would weep for three years, unable to believe that God could ever forgive her for having slandered one of his saints.

Spring came back to the Sault. The new chapel was nearly finished now, and Kateri often wandered over to look at it. One day, as she stood among the chirping congregation of sparrows, filled with wonder and awe that the Creator of all things should be pleased to dwell in a lodge made by the hands of His Indian children, a young woman suddenly came upon her.

Shyly they greeted one another, for they had never met before.

"What is your name?" asked Kateri gently.

"Marie Thérèse."

"Mine is Kateri." I like you, Marie Thérèse, her eyes were saying, as she loked into the stormy face of the Oneida girl. Sorrow and love and fear were there, and hunger and wistfulness, too.

Side by side they stood looking at the church, feeling each other's presence and not knowing just how to begin a conversation.

It was Kateri who broke the silence.

"Which part of the church is reserved for the women?" she asked.

"I think it is over there," said the girl, pointing to the gospel side.

For a moment they were silent again, and then a sudden desire to share the thoughts of her heart with this girl came to Kateri.

"It is not this chapel of wood that pleases God the most," she said. "What He wants above all is to dwell in our hearts."

She did not know—or had she felt it?—that Marie Thérèse had been drawn to the church today because she saw in it the picture of what her heart longed to be—a new, clean lodge for the presence of God. Eagerness and distress were in her bright, burning eyes now fixed on Kateri's face. God is talking to me through this girl, she was thinking. She is holy. I can feel it. She is whole, too, and pure like the Mother of Iesos.

Tears gathered in her eyes and began to roll down her cheeks. How well Kateri understood those tears of repentance, she who thought herself the poorest and least of all God's children.

"I don't deserve to enter this chapel with the others," she continued. "So often I have had the unhappiness of driving God out of my heart that I really deserve to be sent away."

Now Marie Thérèse was weeping bitterly. "You have spoken good words," she sobbed. "I have lived such a dreadful life, Kateri."

Kateri laid a comforting hand on her companion's arm and, leading her to a fallen tree, sat down with her while Marie Thérèse poured out her heart.

What a grim story hers was! An early youth of drunkenness and evil . . . then her conversion in her native village where Father Bruyas had baptized her . . . her constant struggles and failures to resist the firewater . . . the death of her husband.

Again and again Marie Thérèse struggled for words to free herself from the burden of feeling so long frozen up within her. At the end of the story, Kateri took her companion's hand in hers. Silence fell between them, a silence full of understanding and communion and the comfort of shed tears.

The warm spring sunshine beat down, melting the ice in its gentle fires till a thousand little streams, speechless the winter through, found their voices again and sang for sheer ecstasy.

And in Marie Thérèse's soul, set free by the warmth of Kateri's friendship, a new song was preparing, a song for which she would soon discover the words.

12. *Met by Love*

HIGH SUMMER WAS GLOWING ON WOOD AND water and in the eyes of Marie Thérèse as she skimmed over the St. Lawrence River in the canoe. She was full of the joy of taking Kateri on her first visit to the white man's big village of Ville Marie.

"There are so many surprises for you, Kateri," she said eagerly.

"Are there?" said Kateri, feeling safe and secure

with her older friend who was so strong and fearless of new faces and strange new ways.

"You know, the lodges aren't like ours," Marie Thérèse went on. "They are short houses, narrow and tall, and have things like eyes." She laughed. "They look like a lot of old chiefs at a council fire smoking clay pipes. And the palefaces smell so queer! I think it's all the curious things they eat. And . . ."

"There'll be no surprises left for me," laughed Kateri, "if you tell me much more."

"Oh, yes, there will," said Marie Thérèse with an air of mystery.

"Uncle Onsengongo used to say that the palefaces talk very loudly and all at once," said Kateri, "and that their men talk just as much as squaws."

"He was right," said her companion. "It's a good thing they know how to put down their speeches in their queer sign language because if they had to make them up in beads, they'd use up all the wampum in the world and there'd be none left for us!"

Both girls laughed merrily. And then an Indian quietness came between them. No sounds but the soft rhythmic dip, dip, dip of the paddles and the occasional round, bright notes of a bird, like beads strung on long threads of silence.

Ever since the time they had met in front of the new church, Marie Thérèse and Kateri had been fast friends. They shared all their secrets. Together they sought new ways of pleasing God. Together they thought up new ideas for putting love into action, making little rosary chains from wampum, every bead standing for some thoughtful or generous deed to be done between dawn and dusk.

Their very differences had drawn them to one another. Both girls burned with love for God, but each in her own way. "I'm like the torches used for night fishing—all sputter and blaze," Marie Thérèse had once said, "but you're like the quiet candle flame in church, Kateri." Now, as she glanced at her companion's frail body, she remembered this, and a little sadness lingered on her lips as she pictured the virgin white candles before the altar, slowly and silently being consumed by their own clear, steady flame.

At last they came in sight of Ville Marie, the island city of Our Lady, now the great city of Montreal. They left their canoe in the rushes and wandered together into the narrow, quaint streets.

How strange and confusing it all was to Kateri—the horses clip-clopping in front of carts, the French people with their quick, nervous movements, noisy moccasins and excitable, pattering speech. And the squaws! All you could see of them was their faces as they went by, their huge, spreading skirts rustling like dry corn stalks in a breeze.

"There's the market over there," said Marie Thérèse. "That's where Kahriio brings your pretty belts and beadwork when he comes to trade, Kateri."

Kateri made no reply. She felt too much like a fish out of water and would gladly have covered her face with her shawl, so shy did she feel of these strange people with their light, but curious and restless, eyes.

She felt relieved when Marie Thérèse stopped before a little lodge with a cross above it. This was something dear and familiar to her.

They left the busy street for the twilight hush of the chapel. As they knelt down to pray, they heard voices, high and sweet and holy as though coming from some hidden place in the Heart of God.

"Those were the sisters singing," said Marie Thérèse, as they stepped out into the street again and passed through a door in an immense stone wall. "They are white squaws who live here hidden from the world and who spend their whole lives in prayer and praise to Raweniio and in caring for the sick. You see these cabins? The French call a place like this 'God's Lodge.'"

Catching sight of the two Indian girls, a sister in snowy white apron came forward with a warm welcoming smile and greeted them in Iroquois. "I remember you," she said to Marie Thérèse. "Would you like to take your friend inside?"

Kateri's astonishment knew no bounds when she saw the rows and rows of beds. Spellbound, she watched the sisters at their work, charmed by their gay, good humor and their gentle manners as they went from one sick person to another. Mother, Little Brother, Grandfather—she kept seeing them in the sick Indians around her. If only they had had a place like this back in Ossernenon! Before the girls left, the sisters showed them all the nooks and corners of the hospital—the small bakery, the little garden where Sister Bresoles grew plants for medicines. Poor stiff-jointed Grandfather, thought Kateri, and she looked around, half-expecting to see a white flower on one of the plants.

On their way back through the city Kateri heard nothing and saw nothing. Her heart was tuned to the sweet voices in the chapel. Alone, with God alone! How well she understood those sisters! She must found a convent, a poor little lodge in the forest with an oratory like the one she had made on the winter hunting trip.

"Where shall it be?" asked Marie Thérèse, as they talked it over going up the river. She, too, was burning with enthusiasm. Kateri looked across the water at a little blur of green that was the tree-crowned island called Heron. "There," she said, pointing with her paddle. "Oh, Marie Thérèse, won't it be wonderful?"

"It will," said Marie Thérèse, "but shouldn't

we first find out more about the life, Kateri?
I know an older woman who was a patient at
God's Lodge in Quebec. Shall we ask her advice?"

The next day they met Marie Skarichions beneath the big cross by the river. With tears in
her eyes Kateri asked her to keep nothing from
them that could help them live the perfect life.
Marie knew much about the sisters. She told of
their vows of virginity, poverty, and obedience,
of their sacrifices and penances, and of some of the
rules of the cloister.

Nothing could have come closer to Kateri's
own desires. Delighted at the prospect of be-
coming a sister, she invited Marie to join them.
"But first we must be sure that it is the will of
Raweniio," she said. "I'll go and ask the blackrobe what he thinks of it."

Father Cholenec's eyes twinkled as he listened
to Kateri's warm account of life among the Heron
Island sisters. "Ah, my child," he said, "you are
all much too young in the faith for such a scheme.
And besides, just think of all the young men
who would be charmed to visit you on their
way to and from Ville Marie!"

Humbly and obediently Kateri accepted the
refusal. But that day, down by the cross, she
and Marie Thérèse made a solemn and secret
vow—Kateri to remain forever a virgin, Marie
Thérèse never to marry again.

But while Kateri planned for a peaceful life of

prayer and virginity, Katentas was hatching another scheme for her life. "I've been wanting a quiet talk with you for a long time, Kateri," she said one day, slipping her arm in her cousin's and walking along the river bank. "It's about a husband for you."

Kateri's heart sank. Here it was again, the same old story, only now it was even more painful. Now it was a devout Christian woman who was pleading for marriage, and one who had taken her into her home just as Uncle Onsengongo had! There were the same arguments too. Katentas and her husband were growing old. Who would look after Kateri in later years?

Patiently and respectfully Kateri listened to the end. "Thank you, my cousin, for thinking of my welfare," she said gently. "This is such an important matter that I should like time to think it over."

That evening she put her problem before Father Cholenec without telling him of her secret vow.

"You are your own mistress, Kateri," he said. "It is for you alone to decide, but think it over well before refusing."

"Ah, Raguenni!" And the cry came from far back through the years. "It is not possible. I couldn't. I . . ."

"And what will you do for the future?"

The future? What a heavy word! If God could

feed and clothe the little sparrows, couldn't He look after her, too?

"I have no fear of poverty," she said calmly. "My work would bring me in enough for food, and I could always find some rags to clothe myself."

A few days later Kateri told Katentas what she had decided.

"Who ever heard of such a thing?" cried her cousin, now exasperated. "An Iroquois girl unmarried!"

Even Anastasia took sides with Katentas. There were constant little reminders of the joys of marriage and of her own mother's happiness when Kateri was born.

"Dear Mother," said Kateri one day with a playful little smile, "if you found marriage so delightful, why don't you marry again?" And Anastasia, who had all the answers to the catechism, couldn't find any reply to that.

"Think and pray about it for three days, my child," said Father Cholenec when Kateri went to him a second time with her pain of heart.

"Yes, my Father," she said meekly.

If she is still determined, it will be the work of the Holy Ghost, thought Father Cholenec, as he watched her walk slowly away.

Less than fifteen minutes later he heard a soft whisper of moccasins and looked up to see Kateri, shy but resolute, her face alight with joy and peace.

"It's all over, Raguenni," she said. "There is no longer anything to be thought out. I settled the question long ago. You see, I do not belong to myself at all, but to Iesos Cristos."

"Then you love our Lord very much, Kateri?" asked Father Cholenec.

"Father . . . oh, my Father!" A sigh was all that followed, but the half-blind eyes, so quick to laugh and to brim with tears, were filled with the words that she could not find.

On the Feast of the Annunciation of the Blessed Virgin Mary, dressed in a simple blue cloak, Kateri made her vow in the church during Mass. Anastasia and Katentas were among those who were most deeply touched, for Kateri had quite won them by her greatest argument, her radiant holiness. Only her body seemed to remain on earth, and of it she took no care at all.

"Kateri, you should go on the hunting trip with the others. You need the extra food, my child, to give strength to your body," said the blackrobe.

A merry little peal of laughter greeted this remark, and then her face took on the serious, sweet expression it always had when she spoke of spiritual things. "It is true, my Father," she said, "that in the woods the body is treated more delicately, but the soul pines to satisfy its hunger. In the village the body suffers, but the soul finds its delights in Iesos Cristos. Willingly I give this miserable body of mine to starvation and suffering, provided that my soul gets its daily food."

To be poor as her Lord was poor, to know hunger and thirst and pain—this was to live His life and to know His joy and peace.

As each season passed by, Kateri's body grew more feeble. Spring returned to the Sault with its rumors of life and love. Birds preened their feathers till they glistened in the sun, and flew hither and thither on swift wings seeking their mates. Dreaming of their later love-making, the great bull moose rubbed their horns against tree trunks till the velvet dropped off, and then gazed at themselves in water to admire their grey-brown antlers flecked with bronze lights. Young Indian girls greased and combed their hair till it gleamed like a shadowed pool, and hopefully tied red ribbons in it.

But Kateri's pretty hair was always covered now. The small, delicate face, so beautiful in childhood, was sallow and thin. Only the eyes burned with an ever brighter fire. Only the eyes spoke of the hidden treasury of beauty, for, like the King's daughters all glorious within, all her love was winged toward the Great Lover Who looks on the heart alone.

Yet, in spite of her desire to pass unnoticed, it was she more than any other who attracted the

attention of both the savages and the French.
"The miracle of our forests," they called her.
For gradually they had come to realize that she
was a saint, not because of her penances or her
poverty, or for any words she spoke, but because she moved among them like a living ci-
borium, bringing them God's innocence and pity
and peace. Little children, the aged, the sick, and
sorrowful found comfort in her presence. Even
the most devout women tried to get a place next
to her at church because they said that the best
preparation for their own Communion was to
look at Kateri's face.

Never had the people seen even the blackrobes
pray as she prayed. Hour after hour, even in the
freezing cold church, she would remain on her
knees, not praying with her lips nor with her
fingers, but only with her eyes. She came not to
beg God for any favor, nor even for any grace,
but only to adore Him and for the joy of being
with Him.

As her love and joy grew greater, her desire
to suffer grew also. Her failing health alone made
her life a calvary. Often she spent the entire day
stretched on her mat, racked with pain. But it
was not enough, never enough. The love of God
in her was a consuming fire for which she was
forever seeking fuel.

There is always a last spring, a last fullness
and flush to the earth, and one feels its beauty

more when one is very frail. It was the moon of
the new buds. Beneath the cross Kateri sat alone,
thinking of death and the Resurrection, for another Easter was drawing near. Her eyes looked
peacefully over the river, but she did not see it.
She was remembering a scene from her childhood
—a butterfly coming out of its ugly, cumbersome
chrysalis, straining delicate new wings toward the
infinite air and light. That was what death would
be like, leaving the prison house of the body behind. Suddenly her thoughts went back to Gandawagué, to Anidas, the pounding of corn, the
flying pestle. She sat very still while something
precious stirred deep down in her mind and memory groped for it as a diver searches for a pearl
oyster on the ocean floor. "Met by Love . . .
wouldn't you like to be called that, Tekakwitha?"
Ah! What was death but the final and forever
face-to-face meeting with Love?

Full of lightness and joy, she rose to her feet
and walked slowly toward the church. She felt
well today, completely well; there was no pain
anywhere in her body. Inside the church she
fumbled for something around her neck. It was
a little chain of beads, the only one she had kept.
"Would you be willing to give up your pretty
ornaments to imitate the Mother of Iesos?" Anastasia had asked her soon after her arrival at the
mission. Gladly she had put them aside, all but
this necklace. She had not kept it for coquetry,

for she wore it under her dress. She had had it since she was a child. And, after all, would she really be an Indian girl without the touch of beads against the skin? But now this last fragment of herself, this frail but shining link with what was old and familiar and dear to her . . . Lovingly she placed it with other ornaments in the church given by the squaws. Then, kneeling before the tabernacle, she lifted her crucifix to her lips and kissed it fervently, offering her life to God.

The very next day she fell seriously ill. As it was Holy Week, she begged permission to fast.

"Not now," said Father Cholenec. "You have little time left on the earth, my child."

At this news, her face brightened. The final meeting then was not far off!

It was the custom to carry the sick Indians to church on a bark stretcher for their Communion. But because of Kateri's devotion and her extreme weakness, the blackrobes decided to make an exception for her and bring her the Blessed Sacrament.

Touched to the heart that the divine Guest should visit her in her lodge, Kateri was full of joy. But a moment later Marie Thérèse, who seldom left her side now, saw a shadow creep across her face.

"What is it, Kateri?" she asked gently.

"Oh, Marie Thérèse," she whispered, "I have

nothing fitting to wear to receive Him, only these poor rags!"

"I'll lend you my best blouse, Kateri," said Marie Thérèse, and she ran to fetch it, dressing her friend herself and carefully combing her hair.

In the breathless hush of the early morning, with the Indian people reverently following, and the little bell announcing the passage of the unseen Presence, Father Cholenec carried the Blessed Sacrament to Kateri. Her prayer was one long hymn of thanksgiving.

The next day, on Holy Wednesday, after giving her the Blessed Sacrament, Father Cholenec was alarmed to see how feebly her breath came and went. Was it the shadow of death?

"The holy oil for Extreme Unction," he said anxiously, turning to Anastasia, "Send someone to ask Father Chauchetière to bring it. Be quick!"

"Raguenni!" It was Kateri's voice that spoke. "There is no need to hurry. Tomorrow will be soon enough."

Tomorrow—the day celebrating the Feast of Love! Did she know, then, the day of her death?

She knew not only the day, but the very hour. Peacefully the next morning she received Extreme Unction in the presence of the women of the Congregation of the Holy Family. There was a whispering among them afterward. The wood supply to carry them over the feast days must be fetched. Would she last till they got back?

"We can ask her," said one of the women.

Father Cholenec spoke to her for them. "They are so anxious to be with you at the last, Kateri," he explained.

She smiled and nodded. "I shall be here when they return," she assured him.

Around three o'clock in the afternoon, when the last woman had returned and was kneeling beside her—and not until then—did Kateri begin to give up her spirit.

"Iesos, I love Thee!" came the whispered words. Then a long silence. Once again the breath formed words that were almost a sigh, "Iesos . . . Wari." And peacefully, as though falling asleep, Catherine Tekakwitha went forth to meet the Beloved Lover.

But the greatest marvel of all was yet to come. Fifteen minutes later, while Father Cholenec was kneeling in prayer beside her, her face, so marred by illness and mortification, began to change. In the space of a few seconds it became so white and radiant and beautiful that he cried aloud for wonder and astonishment, and all the Indians came running to see the miracle.

Lovingly, tenderly, Anastasia, Katentas and Marie Thérèse dressed her body for burial. Nothing was too good for their Kateri, from the dainty embroidered moccasins to the greased and well-arranged hair.

"See the beautiful girl sleeping!" exclaimed

one Frenchman to another on entering the lodge
some hours later. They did not recognize in the
exquisite face of the dead girl the Kateri they had
known in life. When they were told the story,
they begged to make her coffin themselves, and
they did so in such a way that her face could be
seen to the very last moment.

Amid the tears and sobs of the Indians and
the French, Kateri was buried beneath the great
cross by the river where she had loved to pray.
But her spirit was alive and among them still.
The little crucifix that she wore, the bowl from
which she ate, the very dust from her tomb
worked miracles of healing for the sick who asked
her prayers. And still from far and near pilgrims
come to pray beside her grave, tracing with hopeful eyes the words written on it:

Kateri Tekakwitha
Onkweonweke Katsitsiio
Teotsitsianekaron

The fairest flower that ever bloomed among the
red men.

VISION BOOKS

All Vision Books have full color jackets, black and white illustrations, sturdy full cloth bindings. Imprimatur.